7G

By

Debbie Kump

This is a work of fiction. Names, characters, places, and incidents are products of the author's imagination or are used fictitiously and are not to be construed as real. Any resemblance to actual events, locations, organizations, or person, living or dead, is entirely coincidental.

World Castle Publishing
Pensacola, Florida

Copyright © Deborah Kump 2011
ISBN: 9781937085711
Library of Congress Catalogue Number 2011931711

First Edition World Castle Publishing August 1, 2011
http://www.worldcastlepublishing.com

Licensing Notes

Cover Artist: Karen Fuller
Editor: Beth Price

Dedication

For Doug, my futurist.

Prologue

Paradise Island, Bahamas

"This trip was a lousy idea," Steve Summers grumbled to himself as he looked inside his thin wallet after breakfast. Maybe he'd get lucky in the casino today and break even on the money he'd shelled out for their airfare. And Ellen's unexpected shopping sprees.

The whole thing had been Ellen's idea. The tropical vacation. Their relationship. Everything.

When Steve's ex-girlfriend, Alyssa Kensington, ditched him just before graduation, it didn't take long for her best friend, Ellen Carmikey, to step in. It was a rebound thing, Steve decided. Still, that didn't make it right.

Steve followed Ellen from their hotel room, past the pool and the water slides tunneling through shark tanks, and down to the beach. With a smile, she slipped her arm around his waist. At least she was happy again–the first time in months. Plus, she looked pretty hot in a bikini. Maybe coming to the Atlantis Hotel on the Bahamas' Paradise Island wasn't such a bad idea after all.

"Oh, my God!" Ellen suddenly gagged, covering her nose. "What's that smell?"

Steve crinkled his nose as the reek of overheated cooking oil and putrid meat filled his nostrils.

Craning his head above the forming crowd, Steve spotted a stranded pod of whales on the beach. Ellen clamped her hand over her mouth, her face turning a sickly color of puce. She pushed away from Steve and barreled past the incoming flux of tourists and local residents. News travels fast on a small island.

Steve squinted into the sun, trying to get a better look at the dozen or so creatures lying on the sand, struggling for a breath as their massive weight crushed their own lungs. He wasn't sure what kind of whales they were, but they definitely looked out of place. Their bulbous foreheads and black bodies glistened in the sun–a stark contrast to the white, sandy beach. He leaned in, trying to catch a bit of people's conversations to explain this odd occurrence, when he heard Ellen's desperate cry rise above the clamor of the crowd, "STEVE!"

Of course she expected him to be there for her–one of those relationship obligations, he guessed–but he hoped she'd finish the bulk of her task before he made it back to the room.

Ducking under the low-hanging palm fronds, Steve tailed Ellen at a safe distance. She was nothing like his old girlfriend, Alyssa, he thought with dismay. Alyssa had a stomach of steel. And nerves to boot. Plus she was such a sucker for animals. Why, if Alyssa were here instead of Ellen, she'd probably be organizing the brigade right now, hauling bucket after bucket of seawater to splash across the whales' skin. Not running up to the room, nauseous. Who'd have thought best friends could be so different?

Instead, Alyssa had bolted right after graduation to enlist in the Navy. Wouldn't have a thing to do with Steve. He heard she'd been assigned to work on a submarine, but didn't know much else. She never talked to Ellen anymore, either. Is it because she's jealous? Steve wondered. And still loves me?

Disturbed by losing touch with Alyssa, Ellen had become exceptionally needy and clingy these past few months. So when she suggested they take a week off from classes to head somewhere warm, Steve agreed–but only after finding a sweet deal on last minute airfare and hotel accommodations. Apparently, it wasn't good enough, though. Ellen already blew the backup cash he'd brought along.

Up ahead, Steve watched an old Chevy sedan screech to a halt. Some government official stepped out, hurrying to the scene. He looked piqued for this early in the morning. His harried eyes darted back and forth as he optically typed a message for assistance, no doubt. He raced down the narrow path, accidentally brushing Steve's shoulder as he passed.

"Sorry, mon," the Bahamian official apologized in his classic island cadences.

"No worries," Steve said as he caught a glimpse of the guy's nametag reading, ROY JACKSON, DEPT. OF INTERIOR. Thank God Steve didn't have that job. Cleaning up was going to take a while. And in this hot sun, the smell was bound to get worse.

Ellen opened the door to their hotel room, beckoning desperately, "Steve, hon…a little help?"

"Coming," Steve sighed, though his feet remained rooted to his spot. She probably wants me to hold her hair, he thought with a groan. Sometimes he wasn't sure what he saw in Ellen. Well, he certainly couldn't dump her. Not here. Not now. Their tickets were nonrefundable; the flight back would be unbearable. Better to fake it for a while. Let her down easy once they got home.

Then the door to their hotel room slammed shut. A bright red message from Ellen flashed in front of his eyes: NOW!

Steve sighed again as he trudged to their room. Missing Alyssa.

Chapter One

Medical Office, U.S.S. Siren, Caribbean Sea

"I've got some bad news for you, Seaman Apprentice Kensington," the nuclear submarine's medical officer, Michael Knolls, announced.

Alyssa Kensington winced. She didn't know how much more bad news she could take. Following graduation, she'd spent her entire summer enduring the rigorous submariners' training program at the U.S. Naval Submarine School and the last two months underwater aboard the U.S.S. Siren. All Alyssa wanted was to get off this ship and go back home. Or anywhere on the surface, for that matter. Waking up this morning with red, itchy eyes glued shut was more than she could cope with at the moment. She braced herself for his diagnosis.

"I'll need to take out your DOTS to know for certain. Open wide."

Alyssa forced her goopy eyes open while Medical Officer Knolls scooped out her contact lens-sized, extended wear, virtual computer screen and keyboard eye DOTS. With body heat as the sole catalyst required to power the endothermic chemical reaction recharging each battery, both military and civilians alike constantly wore these Digital Optic/Ophthalmic Transmitters, collectively referred to as "DOTS."

He reached over to unlock a slit lamp from its position on the wall, revolving it into place to examine her retina. Dimming the lights, he instructed her to rest her chin and forehead against the padded head brace.

A blindingly bright vertical beam of light scanned the surface of her cornea. Instinctively Alyssa squinted, shielding her eye from the intense pain, like a torch searing her pupil in two.

Knolls reminded her to look straight ahead at his ear instead of her moth-like tendency to gaze directly into the light itself. He placed his fingers upon her cheekbones, physically keeping the lid open to examine the eye using his biomicroscopic lens.

Alyssa willed her eyes to remain open, resisting the urge to shy away from the extreme contrast once more. The pain was excruciating; her eye socket throbbed as if someone hammered a spike through the back of her skull. Vivid blue spots appeared, interrupting her field of view.

Her previous itchiness no longer seemed unbearable compared to this new form of torture. When would it ever end?

After what seemed an eternity, Knolls flipped off the light. "You can sit back," he finally permitted.

Alyssa watched him secure the slit lamp against the wall to prevent possible damage to the expensive apparatus while the sub was in transit. Then he thoroughly washed his hands in the room's tiny sink. She drummed her fingers impatiently. "So?"

"As I suspected," he confirmed, accidentally bumping the cabinets behind him as he settled into his swivel chair. Knolls folded his arms over his chest. "I'm afraid you have conjunctivitis."

Alyssa narrowed her hazel eyes with uncertainty. Nervously, she ran her fingers through her bobbed brown hair. "Excuse me?"

"Pinkeye," he clarified, rolling his chair as far from his patient as possible within the cramped office.

"Pinkeye?" Alyssa repeated in astonishment. "Am I the first?"

"Yes that I am aware of."

"But...how could that happen?" It made no sense. They'd been at sea too long for symptoms to appear now. "I thought you got it from other people."

"True, but not always. Have you been sick recently? Cold, sniffles, that type of thing?"

Alyssa blinked. How did he know? "A little," she admitted. She hadn't slept much this past week. It was only natural she'd feel a bit run-down.

"Occasionally an upper respiratory tract infection can lead to conjunctivitis. It can flare up pretty quick," Knolls replied as he gazed around the small room–every inch of space filled with essential medical equipment bolted to the wall. Scanning the rows of supply drawers stacked vertically from the floor to the ceiling, he searched for a particular medication. Alyssa could only imagine how he memorized the whereabouts of every item stored inside each locking cabinet.

"So..." Alyssa wondered, raising her eyebrows, "what does that mean?"

Knolls continued, "At this early stage, it's highly contagious. You'll have to be quarantined for the next three days."

Alyssa gasped. He's kidding, right? How would she manage, confined to a minute cubby of a room for that duration? Would claustrophobia inevitably set in? "Isn't there something I can do to control it?" she pleaded.

Sadly, Knolls shook his head. He reached inside the proper drawer, removing a small bottle of sulfacetamide, prescribing, "You'll need to refrain from using your eye DOTS while you administer these drops. Every three hours when you're awake over the next ten days. Even if your symptoms clear sooner, continue to use it for at least two more days. We want to make sure this is properly controlled." He closed the drawer again, locking it in place. "By the way, which rack do you share? I'll make sure your sheets get changed immediately."

"38-F," Alyssa said, frowning. Poor Rosemary. She'd forgotten all about her berthmate. Had she accidentally infected Rosemary as well? Alyssa chastised herself for not having the foresight to remove her pillowcase after she woke with itchy eyes, crusted in residue. It was too late to fix her mistake now–the next shift had already gone to sleep.

Medical Officer Knolls' voice snapped her from her thoughts. "Well, I don't think you'll be wanting these ones again," he chuckled, lightening the mood, as he pitched Alyssa's contagious eye DOTS into the red hazardous waste container affixed to the wall near the sink. Then he tilted her head backward, placing a single medicated drop into each of her eyes. "Blink," Knolls instructed, handing her a tissue to dab the excess.

She sighed in relief as the soothing drops coated her raw, irritated eyes.

"We'll get you some new DOTS in a few days," Knolls continued as he washed his hands again. "You can toss your mobile uplink, too. The next upgrade comes into effect tomorrow, so everyone will be issued new ones anyway. You'll be assigned a fresh set of gear once your quarantine is completed."

Alyssa nodded obediently, dreading her upcoming confinement. Not only would she be missing out on the civilian hoopla of unveiling the latest upgrade to 7G telecommunications technology, she'd be locked up by herself for days...with absolutely nothing for entertainment.

Under the motto, "Run silent, run deep," submarines strove to maintain minimal sound signatures in the water. As a result, they suspended communication with the surface below periscope depth. Alyssa and the other seamen aboard anxiously awaited the national upgrade to 7G Network when the Siren would float a buoy to the surface to make a dangerous, but mandatory, connection with the outside world. The Navy planned to initiate its DOTS' voice amplification program, enabling submariners to speak in a mere whisper that would be audibly transmitted to others nearby–critically important during times of extreme threat.

Seamen were usually limited to communicating with only those aboard the sub. Though during this brief connection period, they'd have the rare luxury of sending messages to loved ones back home. And now Alyssa would miss her chance to contact her mom and old friends. Though she had passed her evaluation for claustrophobic tendencies before being permitted to volunteer as a submariner, she couldn't help but feel a wave of panic grip her throat.

Reluctantly, she removed her chrome mobile uplink from her pocket and peeled the military-issued navy blue stereo DOTS stickers from her outer ear pinnae, tossing them in the refuse bin squirreled in the corner. Without her eye DOTS and MUDE (Mobile Uplink Digital Equipment), she'd have no use for these ear DOTS, either.

On a bare section of stainless steel cabinet, Alyssa noticed a pair of magnetic photos. Desperate for one last stab at conversation before her impending isolation, she asked, "Are those your kids?"

Michael Knolls' face relaxed. Beaming with pride, he nodded. "It's hard to believe how fast they grow up. Lauren's already in fifth grade and Carson's in third. After this tour, I'm heading home for a couple of weeks. Gimme a chance to catch a few of their ball games for a change. Take them to the movies. Just thinking about seeing them again seems to make the time here pass by pretty quick."

Alyssa couldn't help but smile in return. She took another look at the school photos of Lauren and Carson, imagining how excited they'll be to have their father back home again.

"Head to Quarantine," Knolls commanded as he screwed on the lid and handed her the bottle of sulfacetamide drops. "Then every three hours," he reminded her before his eyes began skittering back and forth, optically completing the medical report for the Commander.

Clutching her drops in one hand, she thanked Medical Officer Knolls for his assistance, then released a heavy sigh. Their conversation was briefer than she had hoped. All happiness faded from her body as she stood to leave. Alyssa knew she'd have ample time to spare in her upcoming solitary confinement.

Time to dwell on the myriad thoughts that burdened her mind these past few weeks.

And time to lose her last remaining ounce of sanity.

Chapter Two

Heading for the door, Alyssa frowned, reflecting on what a disaster this "adventure" had turned out to be.

Originally, her plans for the future seemed calculated. Though she swam Varsity all four years of high school and qualified for States in the 200-meter Individual Medley, her grades weren't high enough to guarantee an academic-athletic scholarship at her top three choices: UVa, Virginia Tech, or Old Dominion. And with the tight job market, she didn't want the burden of paying off college loans a decade after graduation.

Granted, Commonwealth Community College was an affordable option, but she needed some space from her ex-boyfriend, Steve Summers, who had already enrolled there in classes this fall. She vowed she wouldn't fall into the same trap as her mom, Linda, by marrying her high school sweetheart. Stuck in the same small town, surrounded by familiar faces her whole life. And where had that gotten her mother? Widowed at age twenty-one with an infant to support after a roadside bomb blasted Alyssa's father's Humvee on his second tour in Afghanistan. Forced to remain in her hometown, working for minimum wage. Never having the opportunity to advance.

Alyssa wasn't like her mother. She longed for adventure.
Something a life with Steve would never provide.

So when a Navy recruiter visited Madison High School in
the spring, promoting the benefits of military service and the
G.I. Bill to defray the rising costs of higher education, Alyssa
decided to enlist. It sounded like the escape she sought. Plus
the experience might actually help her determine what area of
study to pursue in college.

Immediately following high school graduation, Alyssa
departed for the Great Lakes Naval Training Center on Lake
Michigan's western shore. Missing half her friends'
graduation parties, she barely had the opportunity to say
goodbye. But she figured it didn't matter; she'd see them
soon enough on leave.

Upon arriving at the Training Center, Alyssa thrived on
the regimented workout schedule and written examinations.
In fact, it didn't differ much from the challenging AP classes
she took as a senior or the killer practices her old Varsity
swim coach, Mr. Sparks, typically scheduled after they lost a
meet...or whenever he was in a rotten mood.   Every   time
she entered a combat simulation, something in her brain
clicked, sending it into survival mode. Though she ran
outdoor track in high school because she never perfected an
accurate enough throw to make the softball team, her aim in
weapons training was dead-on. At the shooting range, she
could cover all ten bullet holes on her target with a single
silver dollar coin.

Regardless of her weaponry skills, the grueling mental
and physical fatigue required for battle and maintaining her
senses on high alert lacked appeal for Alyssa. So with her
physical stamina, drive to succeed, and intrigue with life
below the surface–plus the Navy's acceptance of women on
subs for the first time in history — she readily volunteered to

become a submariner. Alyssa took her rigorous screening in stride, viewing everything as a game not much different than Coach Sparks' infamous workouts she'd endured to achieve her goal of going to States. Then she was sent to the Naval Submarine School New London in Groton, Connecticut for additional training where she learned the ins and outs of the job she'd perform over the next four years.

By the end of the summer, Alyssa had risen from the rate of Seaman Recruit to Seaman Apprentice Kensington. She was stationed on the United States Ship Siren, the second member of the Hydra class of attack submarines–a class so secretive the Secretary of Defense had not yet announced their arrival to the general public (despite taxpayers footing the $3 billion price tag per ship). Here, she would be part of the team of submariners conducting a series of classified sonar tests in the Atlantic Ocean and Caribbean Sea.

True, Alyssa felt slightly guilty for leaving her mother alone back home with only their golden retriever, Tucker, for company. But Alyssa was compelled to ensure the security of her future. She needed an impressive resume to attract future employers — one that would make her stand out from the long list of applicants vying for the limited positions available. Something that living at home and attending community college could not guarantee.

Although the first month was an adjustment, Alyssa had coped well with the cramped living spaces and lack of privacy aboard a nuclear submarine. Yet her recent infatuation with Officer Hidalgo complicated the situation. Compounded with the deadly testing exercise she conducted yesterday, Alyssa had really begun to resent her decision to volunteer for the U.S.S. Siren.

Chapter Three

Ducking through the rounded opening of the small watertight door joining the Medical Office and the hallway, Alyssa tried to avoid bumping her head or knees on its hard, metal edges. She hesitated momentarily outside, blinking to allow her naked eyes to readjust to the dimly lit hall. And with great difficulty, she resisted the urge to rub her eyes clean to improve her visual clarity.

It felt extremely odd for Alyssa to function with normal, unaided eyesight. Since the military's invention of night vision mode had been incorporated into the eye DOTS last year, the Navy found they could reduce energy usage by dimming the red lighting required in regions devoted solely to foot traffic. The night vision product was not yet available for civilian use, but the military utilized the innovation regularly. Now the Navy reasoned all submariners could see their surroundings clearly as the mode automatically took effect with insufficient lighting—albeit everything appeared bathed in an eerie greenish tint, like something from a B-movie horror flick. Though Alyssa merely used her night vision capabilities to assist her in safely navigating from one part of the ship to another without collision, she imagined the Marines stationed to regions of conflict within the perpetually war-torn areas of the Middle East found the night vision and infrared heat signature modes highly effective in locating their enemies…and in ensuring their own survival.

However, without her eye DOTS in place right now, Alyssa felt blind. She reached out, searching for the wall as she crept down the narrow, darkened passageway to locate her meager belongings. Wary, she inched forward along the grated metal floor. Normally, she could see straight through the steel grates to other seamen working on decks below. But without the DOTS, the lower decks appeared utterly black, like a bottomless chasm beneath her feet.

Though the doctor's office was positioned just down the hall from crew quarters, her laborious effort made it seem more like they were on opposite ends of the ship. Step after cautious step, she stole past the berthing areas of closet-sized rooms containing triple-stacked racks with privacy curtains for sleeping nine enlisted men at a time. Since submariners adjusted their routines to fit into an 18-hour schedule— usually six on, twelve off—each berth was shared, easily accommodating eighteen men over the course of a typical day underwater.

However, Alyssa and the other women onboard were segregated from the men for privacy issues. And as this was one of the first subs to set sail with female submariners, they grouped the women together in a less desirable location- squeezed into the crannies of the Torpedo Bay. She knew she shouldn't complain; they had their own private head. And a mattress to claim. Often, Alyssa found exhausted submariners curled up directly on the metal, grated floor. Alyssa always slept comfortably until awakened by her berthmate, Rosemary Dela Cruz, on the next shift. At least she had…until this past week. How could she sleep when thoughts of that illicit night spent with Officer Hidalgo corrupted her mind?

Despite her arduous progress and stopping regularly to back against the wall as others overtook her, she finally managed to reach the Torpedo Bay in the bow of the ship. The overhead emergency lighting's thin red beams reflected off the polished finish of the torpedoes' hulls. In the dim gleam, Alyssa extended her arms, searching for the uprights of the first set of racks sandwiched between the rows of torpedoes.

In the darkness, she overestimated the distance and stubbed her shin against the lowest rack jutting out into the aisle. Doubling over, Alyssa grabbed her leg, cursing under her breath. A nearby sleeping seaman grunted before rolling over on her mattress. Alyssa gritted her teeth, whispering a strained, "Sorry," as she rubbed the rapidly forming bruise. Then she limped forward, hand over hand toward her rack between the second and third rows of torpedoes. All the while, she forced herself to restrain from touching her unbearably itchy eyes and spreading germs to every surface she groped.

Upon reaching her rack, she glanced down at the shadowed lump of Seaman Apprentice Rosemary Dela Cruz's dozing form. She rarely saw her berthmate since dining space onboard the Siren was so limited and they worked at different stations. Their meager exchanges consisted of a few garbled words while Alyssa dragged her bleary-eyed body off the thin mattress, allowing Rosemary the cherished opportunity to rest.

Guilt consumed Alyssa for contracting conjunctivitis in the first place. With the pathogen as contagious as Medical Officer Knolls had described, she felt horrible for Rosemary whose cheek pressed against the contaminated pillowcase, her thick black hair spilling in waves as she unsuspectingly slept.

Medical Officer Knolls was justified in quarantining her.

An outbreak would undoubtedly occur if this disease were not immediately contained.

To avoid further disturbing Rosemary and the two sleeping seamen stacked above her, Alyssa carefully slid open the sturdy storage pan beneath the rack to remove her small bag of toiletry items, knowing she couldn't return here until the end of her quarantine.

The trip back to the Quarantine Room felt like a walk-of-shame. Alyssa imagined she wore a bright red "Q" embroidered upon her chest, as recognizable as the pus accumulating in the corners of her red eyes. Granted, the submariners she passed were more likely engaged with one of the numerous sources of entertainment available through the DOTS and supporting mobile uplink technology, it seemed each gaze bore directly upon her.

She kept her head down, avoiding eye contact. Each time she encountered someone, she turned sideways, standing at attention with her back pressed firmly against the wall, allowing the other seamen and officers to pass unobstructed through the narrow corridors.

"S.A. Kensington? Why aren't you at your station?"

Crap.

Alyssa froze, recognizing the voice of authority immediately. Why did she have to bump into him, of all people?

Chapter Four

Slowly, Alyssa spun around to salute the commanding dive officer from her shift. "Sorry I won't be there today, Officer Hidalgo," she replied, diverting her eyes in embarrassment. "I was sent to Quarantine." With head hung low, she continued her laborious journey down the hall.

She had only advanced a few steps when she felt him grasp her forearm, wheeling her to face him. "Alyssa," Officer Hidalgo asked, his tone softer now, "are you alright?"

Alyssa shrugged in response as she peeked upward, attempting to gauge his expression. Was he sorry that her crewmates would have to do additional work in her absence? Or did he seem genuinely concerned about her? Since last week, she'd spent countless hours overanalyzing his actions at the Mess Hall, unsure of his true feelings toward her.

"About earlier. I should've stood up for you, Alyssa. But I—"

"Didn't want to make waves," she finished for him in a deadpan voice. "I understand."

Justin was career. And she was just using this experience to help pay her college bills down the road. Did she actually think he'd speak up in front of the XO–the Executive Officer, second in command–when she expressed concern over the unexpected whale strandings in the Bahamas following their recent sonar testing? The test that she had conducted. In her heart, she knew the two incidents were linked. Too many different species had beached themselves to be deemed coincidental.

Worse, their next active sonar test was only a few days away. She couldn't disobey her orders by refusing to comply; training instilled her to follow the chain of command without question. Nor could she live with herself for causing more deaths of innocent marine life, not after she'd spent months listening to the natural noises of the ocean: humpback whale songs, dolphin clicks, even snapping shrimp. But when she mentioned her concerns to her superiors aboard the Siren, they readily dismissed her.

And Justin Hidalgo had watched the entire conversation. Without uttering a word in her defense.

At least she knew where his loyalty lay. In self-preservation. Then why jeopardize losing his commission by getting involved with her?

Unless he didn't think he'd get caught.

Alyssa knew the Navy frowned upon relationships between seamen of different rates, the naval equivalent of military rank. Yet she couldn't resist Dive Officer Justin Hidalgo's infectious smile, his upbeat disposition, or his charming personality. Even the military's standard high-and-tight buzz cut looked stunning on him. He was far more mature in appearances and behavior than any of the guys she'd dated back in high school, especially Steve Summers. Plus Justin Hidalgo was one of the few people onboard who'd paid her any personalized attention since she'd arrived. Naturally, the other enlisted men and women spend the majority of their free time accessing the variety of sources of virtual entertainment–movies, games, eBooks, and music.

Why not, when everyone wore DOTS and mobile uplinks continuously throughout the tour of duty?

At first, Alyssa had been preoccupied with those distractions as well. Yet basic training demanded intense amounts of physical exertion, leaving Alyssa too exhausted to keep up with her old friends on a daily basis. But once she found out that Ellen Carmikey ("The Backstabber") had started dating Steve ("The Self-absorbed Jerk"), Alyssa stopped replying to their text messages altogether. Wasn't it taboo to hook up with your best friend's ex?

Alyssa didn't care that Ellen and Steve had loads in common–music, sports, movie genres–not to mention they both lived at home this year and took classes at Commonwealth Community College. With the Siren's limited communications to the outside world, she had no choice but to disassociate herself from the small-town gossip in quaint Madison, Virginia, nestled against the backdrop of the Blue Ridge Mountains. She'd wanted a different life.

And this was how she would pay for it.

But Alyssa often felt empty; as if a part of her soul longed for sights and possessions she couldn't have with the choices she'd made for her future.

Justin Hidalgo filled that void in her life. He was considerate. Sweet. Interesting.

It would've been wonderful…if she weren't consumed with trepidation of ruining his career.

"It's just pinkeye," Alyssa told Officer Hidalgo, finding her voice at last. "I guess I'll be out of commission for a few days."

"Oh." He recoiled as he made the connection between her bloodshot eyes and the infamous disease. His expression turned blank and formal as he stiffened abruptly.

Alyssa frowned, chiding herself, What did I expect? That he'd actually miss me while I was gone? Don't be absurd, Alyssa.

Then she detected the sound of footsteps approaching as another submariner rounded the corner. Alyssa's heart thumped rapidly inside her chest while her cheeks flushed hot. Instinctively, she and Justin stepped away from each other with their backs flat against the wall, allowing the submariner to pass by unobstructed.

This crewman didn't appear concerned. But eventually, someone would.

From the bottom of her knotted stomach, Alyssa dreaded the day their secret got out, wondering if Justin felt the same concern. How could he not? she reasoned. His future is at stake.

"Well, cheer up, Kensington," said Hidalgo, maintaining formalities in the event of a repeated interruption. "I s'pose I'll see you back in a couple of days, then." His lips turned into a grin that illuminated his eyes. With a casual wave, he headed back down the hall toward the Command and Control Room.

Alyssa stood rooted to her spot, catching her breath. Though only a week had passed since they'd last been together, it felt like a month. How could she possibly keep this hushed for the remainder of their tour? Especially when his mere presence affected her so strongly? She had to stop blushing every time she bumped into him. Her feelings were too obvious to any onlooker.

That settles it, Alyssa decided. I'd better end things before this gets out of hand.

Unfortunately, that was easier said than done. She knew deep within the confines of her heart that it was too late to break things off.

She was already in love.

Composing herself once more, Alyssa hurried down the last few sets of darkened hallways, hoping to avoid additional injury. Fortunately, she didn't bump into another soul she knew en route to her assigned destination. In fact, she was almost grateful to near the Quarantine Room.

Until she stood before its door.

Alyssa couldn't believe some people actually enjoyed being quarantined to avoid work; like a vacation from the regimen of sub life for a few days. Rather, she felt deeply ashamed for being incapacitated. Forcing others to work harder in her absence.

She stared at the engraved gold letters spelling QUARANTINE on the plaque bolted to the door. How many times had she passed by, almost mocking those inside for becoming quarantined? It wasn't like the Navy hadn't set precautions in place. No one went anywhere barefoot; shower shoes minimized the spread of athlete's foot. And seasickness patches were readily available for the times they surfaced in rough seas. But below depths of 350 feet, not even the turbulence generated from a hurricane above could toss the sub, so few submariners (herself, included) bothered to use the patches during the majority of the trip.

Entering the miniscule room, Alyssa's heart sank. And she'd thought the Medical Office was confining!

No floor space of the Quarantine Room was left unoccupied. A single, extra thin and abnormally stubby pull-down berth lay squeezed between the metal wall and the head. She could only use the saltwater head with the bed stowed away. Alyssa had to scramble onto the mattress to even shut the door behind her. Plus the new Hydra class relied entirely on the DOTS for daily announcements, eliminating the need for flat screen monitors, even in Quarantine.

She gazed into the mirror, disgusted by her appearance, embarrassed by her heart-driven actions, and disturbed by the unnecessary deaths she had caused. Dropping onto the tiny mattress in despair, she sat on her hands to suppress the burning desire to rub her eyes.

Three days.

With absolutely nothing to do but dwell upon circumstances that were beyond her control.

How did this happen to me? Alyssa wondered. I let my defenses down for a second and end up falling for some guy. And not just any guy, but an officer. What was I thinking?!

She frowned. And what will he think of me if I ruin his career?

Unable to restrain her emotions any longer, contaminated tears rolled off her cheeks, washing away her grief.

Chapter Five

Coombs Science Center, Southern Florida State University, Miami Springs, Florida

"Blasted outdated technology!"

Simon Greene, Associate Professor of Marine Biology, muttered a string of obscenities under his breath as the screen of his Smart Board froze for the third time this morning. He glanced at the clock on his DOTS, a muted lime green display in the upper corner of his right periphery. At this rate he'd never finish his lecture notes in time.

He restarted the computer again, drumming his fingers impatiently while the screen buzzed to life. This entire process would be far easier if only the University permitted him to purchase the software to prepare the Power Point Presentation on his DOTS and interface with the students directly. But that would allow non-matriculated students access to his notes–and the Southern Florida State University had its monetary interests at stake. Though Simon knew that 7G's recording capabilities would make this a challenge to monitor for much longer.

Perhaps if the University devoted a fraction of its million dollar alumni donations to improving his Department's high-end data processing programs, the wasted hours fine-tuning lecture notes on a desktop computer or fumbling around with an outdated mouse and manual keyboard wouldn't prove as frustrating. Or deduct as much precious time that could be better spent securing another grant to fund his research in toothed whale communication and echolocation.

The next American telecommunications upgrade to 7G Network–allowing instantaneous optical and audio recording through the DOTS and smaller MUDEs–proved promising. Simon anticipated interacting directly with a dolphin's brain to view the dark, murky underwater world through sound waves. Only a few days remained before he could test his software with the new system. But he couldn't afford to think about that now.

Simon glared out his office window at the new Cyclones football stadium under construction. Twin Bobcats rumbled over uneven terrain, dragging dirt across the spacious field and flattening it to a perfect grade. Contractors had trucked in and replanted mature palm trees around the outside perimeter of the stadium. A crane towered above, its mobile arm swinging rows of bleacher seats into position. Deluxe box seats circled the upper row, each luxuriously furnished. And to think of the innovations and educational resources his department could enjoy at the cost of one of those boxes alone!

With a sigh, Simon returned his attention to the screen, the blinking cursor signaling its readiness to proceed. He double clicked on the Power Point icon to resume typing his notes when a bright red light suddenly flashed in the left side of Simon's field of view. The mobile uplink inside his pocket vibrated, expressing a similar, irritated tone. An urgent call.

Simon rolled his eyes. "What now?" he grunted, directing his gaze to the incessant, pulsating red light in his eye DOTS.

A name appeared in the air, as if each letter floated somewhere in space between Simon's pupils and the computer monitor: ROY JACKSON, BAHAMAS DEPARTMENT OF THE INTERIOR.

What lousy timing. Simon rapidly flicked his eyes to focus on the keyboard application icon in the lower left area of his field of view. A virtual keyboard materialized in space, accessible through the blink of an eye. Glancing at the letter G, then O, he spelled his response.

While waiting for Roy's reply, Simon perused his catalog of images on the computer's hard drive—folders of digital photos he'd taken over the years while researching whales in various parts of the United States—trying to decide which ones he wished to include in today's lecture on his specialty: toothed whale communication.

Bold scarlet letters appeared in front of Simon's retinas, directly over a picture of a Pacific Northwest pod of orcas pack-hunting a significantly larger baleen whale. WE HAVE A SITUATION.

Simon's eyes darted over the DOTS's spatial keyboard quickly as he typed his response with a mere glance in the direction of each desired key: NOT A GOOD TIME, ROY. Using the desktop's mouse, he rapidly scanned through five more photos until he found the one of the orca pod he'd been looking for.

Roy's message returned, the red letters insistent: PICK UP.

"I don't have time for this," Simon grumbled, peeking at the phone icon hovering in the lower right of his peripheral vision. Immediately his ear DOTS—the sticker electronics attached to his outer ear pinnae—hummed, transmitting the familiar intonations.

It'd been a few months since they last spoke, but Roy's melodious Bahamian accent was unmistakable, as if every word he uttered went to the tune of a Caribbean song. While roommates their freshman year at Dartmouth, Roy's voice had made the girls in their co-ed dorm swoon…and prompted Simon to struggle phasing out his own nasally tone. Now, ten years later, Dr. Greene could easily pass for a resident of Upstate New York, instead of someone born and raised in the town of Little Neck on the North Shore of Long Island.

"How soon can you get here?" Roy Jackson asked, his voice pleasantly lilting up and down, despite the gravity of the news he bore.

"Listen, Roy. I'm right in the middle of something," Simon replied gruffly, dragging his fingers down his prematurely graying goatee. "Can't you get someone else?"

"I've already contacted everyone else in the area. You're our last resort."

Grabbing a fistful of his deep brown hair, Simon released a heavy sigh. Roy probably needed his guidance with another case of Red Tide or Portuguese Man-of-War infiltrating the beaches. Barely heeding Roy's lengthy response, Simon surfed through his catalog of photographs, eager to complete his task now that the computer was cooperating again. Yet, Roy's haggard voice described a series of unexplained mass strandings beginning early this morning on several different beaches of New Providence and Paradise Islands.

Simon's face turned white, his finger pausing on the mouse. Impossible. He must have misheard his old roommate. "How many did you say?"

"Two beaked, eleven pilots, and a spinner."

Simon reclined in his chair, unable to believe his ears. Why would so many whales strand on the same day? And from different species, no less? Sure, entire pods of pilot whales often beached themselves, either refusing to abandon an ailing leader or becoming confused by unfamiliar shoreline contours caused by storms or rising tides. But beaked whales and a spinner dolphin stranding at the same time, too? Something wasn't right.

"Fine. I'll catch the next plane out. Meet you in Nassau." Simon grabbed his navy blue backpack, reliably stuffed with essentials. Regardless of the fact that there were other qualified marine biologists residing in South Florida or that Simon's focus was in communication, not mammalian physiology, Roy Jackson always contacted him in an emergency. And recently, these emergencies had been occurring with unusual regularity. He'd have to wait until he saw the victims to determine the exact cause.

But Simon had his suspicions as to who was to blame.

And they'd pay for their damages. He would guarantee that.

Chapter Six

"Sweet!" Erik Weber grinned as he read the scrawled writing on the sign attached to the door of Lecture Hall 201 in the Coombs Science Center. "Class is cancelled today!"

He knew he should take Dr. Greene's Intro to Marine Bio course more seriously–with his sister, Kristen, the teaching assistant and all–but lately he'd been letting it slide. She shouldn't take it personally. He'd been letting everything slide.

That's easy to do when you've got a distraction. And Rachael Gallagher proved the best distraction of all.

Besides, he wasn't like Kristen. She'd been obsessed with marine animals ever since their parents brought them to SeaWorld in Orlando that first time back in elementary school. For years, she dreamed of becoming a dolphin trainer, teaching her stuffed animals tricks and flips. But as she got older, her focus changed. She became fascinated with the innate intelligence of these animals rather than using them for entertainment. It was natural she'd want to come to the U of M for grad school to study under Dr. Greene.

Though sometimes Erik wished she'd gone someplace else. With her here, it felt like she watched his every move. Especially when he was with Rachael.

"Erik? Where're you going?"

The sound of his name broke his thoughts. Erik spun around, readily spotting the wavy red hair and freckled face of his roommate, Lucas Jenkins, walking down the hall.

"Class's cancelled," he informed Lucas. Though they weren't the best of friends, they tolerated living together in their small, double room well enough. And since this was the only class they shared, Erik usually sat by him in lecture. But Erik had stopped studying with him back at their dorm. Especially after Lucas aced their last exam while Erik scraped by with a C-minus.

"Cancelled?" Lucas turned around and walked out the building with Erik. "Did Kristen say why?"

What a nerd, Erik thought. He actually sounds disappointed. "Nope. Didn't see her. Dr. Greene was probably busy getting ready for the upgrade. She said he's got some new research proposal that's linked to the 7G Network."

"Huh." Erik imagined Lucas was trying to imagine what dolphins and 7G visual and audio recording capabilities could possibly have in common. Not that Erik could tell him. Kristen had kept the whole project pretty hushed.

"So...where're you headed now?"

Erik shrugged, tossing his long, sandy blonde bangs out of his eyes. "Not sure, really. Now I've got nothing 'til lunch. I'm supposed to meet Rachael and her cousin at the dining hall today."

"Her cousin? Who's that?"

"I dunno. Jamie or something. She's a prefrosh checking out the campus, I guess." Erik suddenly felt compelled to add, "It'll probably be boring, though. Bet they'll spend the whole time talking about clothes."

Lucas chuckled. "Hate to break this to you, man, but you're whipped."

"Am not," Erik retorted. Though the defensiveness in his own voice surprised him. Was he whipped? Erik brushed off the comment. His roommate didn't have a girlfriend; he didn't know what it was like. Changing the subject, he asked Lucas, "What're you gonna do now?"

"Think I'll head over to the courts and shoot some hoops."

That shouldn't have surprised Erik. Lucas always played pick-up basketball when he got the chance. How he managed to get such good grades was beyond Erik, not to mention quite infuriating at times.

"Cool. Maybe I'll join y-" Erik stopped short. Partway across the quad, he spotted Rachael. With another guy.

"D'you know him?" Erik asked Lucas as he nodded toward a tall, muscular guy with dark skin, a chiseled face, and short black hair hidden beneath his fitted baseball cap. The guy was huge compared to Erik. Probably a football player. Linebacker type. And he was hugging his girl.

"Never seen him before. But sorry, man," Lucas said, giving Erik a sympathetic smile, "he's out of your league."

Real comforting, Erik thought, coming from his roommate who knew him better than most on campus. Except for Rachael. And Kristen, of course. But she didn't really count.

"I think I'll meet you down there," Erik said, quickly changing direction to avoid passing Rachael. He ducked behind the corner of the nearest building to get a second peek. Her intensely blue eyes twinkling, Rachael flashed the guy a wide grin. Then she slipped her arm through his and led him down the sidewalk. Her straight blonde hair swayed mockingly across the middle of her back with each lighthearted step.

Erik blinked, watching her leave. Why was Rachael cheating on him? And how long had this been going on?

Chapter Seven

Southern Florida State University off-campus housing

"Not again!" Kristen Weber groaned as she ran from the kitchen table, leaving her breakfast half-eaten. Clamping one hand over her mouth, she flew down the hall to the bathroom, locking the door behind her. She managed to lift the toilet seat lid seconds before her gag reflex struck. Kristen winced as undigested oatmeal splashed inside the porcelain basin. Pulling her curly blonde hair back against the nape of her neck, she bent over the bowl a second time. Her stomach heaved until gastric acid burned the lining of her esophagus and the back of her throat. Who knew something as bland as oatmeal could prove so unsettling? She flushed the toilet, ridding the room of the pungent odor.

Yet the acrid taste of bile lingered in her mouth. Kristen wiped her lips with the back of her hand, and waited, ensuring her queasiness had passed. This was the third day in a row. What could possibly be wrong with her?

She checked her forehead to test for fever, but didn't feel flushed. Besides, she'd already gotten the flu shot this year. After waves of student deaths swept college campuses across the nation from the swine and bovine influenza outbreaks in the past, Southern Florida State University mandated that every student visit the school's medical center to receive an annual flu shot before enrolling in courses. Besides, the last two days Kristen felt normal by lunchtime. Surely if she were ill, the symptoms would persist through the remainder of the day, wouldn't they?

On wobbly legs, Kristen righted herself by the sink, studying her face in the mirror. Her normal tanned complexion seemed oddly pale today, almost a sickly color of puce. Even the dark circles under her eyes had become more pronounced. Of course, she'd had little time for relaxation these days. The summer seemed ages ago, when she'd spend long days at the beach hanging out with her boyfriend, Dane Whistler, then working odd jobs at night to pay the rent.

Now that the semester had started up, Kristen couldn't afford such pleasures. Simon Greene was on the breakthrough of a major discovery and mandated all grad students pull long hours in the lab. In reality, the extra time she devoted to research helped distract her from thoughts of Dane. As difficult as it was to admit, things between them just weren't the same anymore.

Kristen knew their long distance relationship was bound to be rocky. Despite the ability to readily text each other throughout the day using their DOTS, it was inevitable they'd eventually lose touch. With the National Conversion to 7G happening this fall, Dane predicted this was his best opportunity to be on the cutting edge of the telecommunications market. So he accepted an internship with a start-up company called Dreamscape based in Washington, D.C. The money wasn't great, but he hoped the experience would land him a high-paying job, perhaps within the company itself. The CEO of Dreamscape expected their new patent on optical dream recording to generate trillions in advertising revenues alone as the nation uploaded their dreams free of charge. Dane's computer science degree and ingenuity made him a perfect fit. Dreamscape chose him from a pool of hundreds of other qualified applicants.

When Dane came back to visit Kristen at the U two weeks ago, they tried to pick their relationship up right where they'd left off. Yet things were different this time. Everything seemed forced: their conversations, their kisses…everything. Had they really drifted apart that much? Perhaps it was all the time he'd spent with his colleagues in D.C. that had changed him, diverting his love toward money and power instead of her. With tears in her eyes, Kristen kissed him goodbye at the airport, confident he wasn't going to miss her as much as she would him.

Since then, she'd barely heard from Dane. His replies to her texts were brief and rushed. Kristen wasn't sure if he was truly too busy to talk or if he'd simply lost interest. Whenever she texted him, she deliberated over every word she wrote, her eyes lingering on each key…only to delete them all and start anew. She spent sleepless nights wondering if she'd become dependent on him, clinging to memories of their glorious summer together. Now he acted more like a stranger than a boyfriend.

On the outside, she wore a strong face, hiding from her roommates the nightly tears that soaked her pillowcase. And as close as she and her brother, Erik, had been growing up, somehow she didn't feel comfortable confiding in him now. He'd probably tell her she was only overanalyzing everything. (He'd psychoanalyzed everything she said since completing Psych 101 last fall.) Besides, these days he seemed more preoccupied with his budding relationship with Rachael. In a way, it was cute to see him so lovesick for the first time in his life. On the other hand, seeing them joined at the hip proved quite nauseating at times.

Especially when Kristen felt so alone without Dane.

Bending over the sink, Kristen splashed cool, soapy water across her face. The soothing water cleansed her pores and washed away her conflicted emotions. Sliding her hand towel off the rack, she dabbed her cheeks and forehead dry. She grabbed her toothpaste from the medicine cabinet, liberally applying it to her brush and meticulously scrubbing the vile taste from her mouth. Refreshed, Kristen returned her toothpaste to the medicine cabinet, placing it carefully on top of her round case of pills.

Then Kristen gasped, pressing her hand to her mouth. In a horrifying way, everything suddenly made sense.

Her pills.

Popping open the circular case, she blinked in disbelief. Kristen wrapped her arm around her belly, fending off another bout of nausea…though not food-induced this time.

Only one yellow placebo remained and she still hadn't gotten her cycle.

She'd never been this late before.

Chapter Eight

Crystal Court, Atlantis Hotel, Paradise Island, Bahamas

"Unbelievable," Steve Summers muttered under his breath. You'd think Ellen had enough swimsuits packed to survive the last afternoon of their trip. Yet instead of testing his luck in the casinos again, Steve found himself waiting outside another dressing room to give Ellen feedback on her latest bikini selection. "I just have to have that one!" she declared as they passed by the Gucci window display of the Atlantis' Crystal Court. His heels dug into the floor as she dragged him inside.

Alyssa never would've subjected me to this kind of torment, Steve thought as he glanced at his watch, shifting it on his wrist to expose the white band of skin hidden underneath. If nothing else, at least he got a good tan on this trip. Meanwhile, his money, time, and relationship had all gone to pot. Not to mention he'll have loads of work to catch up on from skipping out of classes for a week. Why did he ever let Ellen talk him into coming to the Bahamas?

The handle on the dressing room door turned slowly.

"Finally," Steve groaned, rolling his eyes. It doesn't matter how good it looks, just give her a quick 'no,' he reminded himself. Sure, she'd be pissed for a while, but she'd get over it. He'd already seen this price tag and knew his wallet couldn't bear much more abuse.

"What do you think?" Ellen asked. Pushing the door open wide, she spun a slow circle in front of Steve.

The black string bikini caught the fluorescent lighting, shimmering as she turned. It rode low across her hips and tight across her chest, leaving little to the imagination. Steve swallowed hard. His eyes widened as his brain went blank, immediately forgetting his resolve to reject it no matter what. With eyebrows peaked high on his forehead, he released a low whistle, a dazed expression forming across his face. And here he thought she'd looked hot before.

"Well?" Ellen placed her hands on her hips, her mouth turning into a pout. "What do you think?" she repeated.

Steve quickly glanced over each of his shoulders. The store appeared nearly empty, its retailer preoccupied with helping the few shoppers purchase their selections. Without a word, Steve stepped inside the dressing room, locking the door behind him.

Ellen's face registered surprise. "What are you doin...."

But Steve silenced her question by placing his mouth firmly against hers, shaping it to his will. His hands sought her skin, eager to hold her close to his body. His fingers traveled up her bare spine until she shivered with pleasure. He loved it when she did that.

Then a small voice rang out inside his head, What about Alyssa? I thought you were ready to dump Ellen as soon as you got back.

We're not back yet, Steve thought. His arms wound tightly across Ellen's back, his fingers sliding through her silky blonde hair as he kissed her harder yet. Besides, why should he sacrifice what he already has without knowing whether Alyssa would even take him back?

Chapter Nine

Southern Florida State University off-campus housing

The door opened. Kristen Weber looked up from her spot on the couch and watched her younger brother enter the house. He never knocked.

"Sick again?" Erik asked, looking unusually piqued himself.

Kristen froze, not realizing he'd noticed her condition these past few days. Could he possibly suspect anything? Nah. She'd only figured it out; plus nothing was certain yet. She could just be late. For the first time ever. Trouble was, she had difficulty convincing even herself.

"Don't you think you should get checked out at the clinic?" Erik asked, tossing his backpack onto the floor. He plopped down next to her on the couch. "It could be one of those new flu strains."

Kristen shook her head. "I'll be fine."

He eyed her skeptically.

Erik seemed unusually perceptive today. Ever since he'd met Rachael, he'd been so infatuated with his girlfriend that he hardly noticed Kristen. But today he seemed sullen. "Something wrong?" she wondered.

44

Erik shrugged, crossing his arms over his chest as he slouched further into the couch. His long blonde bangs fell limp across his face.

Fine, don't answer. She had loads on her own mind that she wasn't exactly ready to share with him, either.

But after a few minutes of awkward silence, Erik lifted his head to ask, "Heard from Dane lately?"

Thanks for rubbing it in, Kristen thought. "Not so much. But he's probably super busy right now anyway."

Why did she feel compelled to make excuses for him? To hide the fact their relationship had turned rocky? "How's Rachael doing?" she added, bracing herself for Erik's blissful reply. Sometimes it was enough to make her sick.

Instead, Erik blurted the whole story of how he'd discovered Rachael with another guy.

"Oh, Erik!" Kristen wrapped her arm tenderly around his shoulder, pulling him toward her for comfort like she did when they were kids. "Are you sure?"

Erik nodded, brushing his bangs from his face. Kristen thought she caught him sniffle once. Something he'd never do in front of the guys. Things were different when it was your sister.

She placed one hand over his. "I'm so sorry. Love sucks, doesn't it."

"You said it," Erik agreed. Then his gray eyes turned distant. They quickly scanned from left to right, reading a text on his eye DOTS, no doubt. His expression turned sour.

"Was that her?" Kristen dared to ask.

Erik's face fell into his hands. "Can you believe it? She still wants me to meet her for lunch!"

"She didn't see you, I take it."

Without looking at her, Erik shook his head. Kristen patted his back, unable to think of anything to say.

Leaning back against the couch, she sighed deeply, wishing Dane would send her a text. Just a single word to acknowledge her existence. But the only thing moving on her eye DOTS' virtual screen was the clock blinking 10:30 A.M.

10:30 A.M.?

Kristen shot off the couch. "Why aren't you in class?" she said in a condescending tone.

"Easy, Mom," Erik snipped. "I should be asking you the same question. Didn't you know? Greene cancelled lecture today."

"Oh. Right." Kristen sat back down, and directed her attention to her email icon. Then she rifled through her list of emails to find a message from Simon Greene. Why hadn't he asked her to cover for him? Didn't he trust her enough to teach a bunch of undergrads?

Finally, Kristen found the email she'd been looking for. It was brief to the point of curtness. Just like Simon. Kristen read, SITUATION IN BAHAMAS. BE BACK TOMORROW.

Talk about being vague. Of course he'd be back tomorrow. Simon would never dream of missing the unveiling of 7G.

"News to you?" Erik asked, one eyebrow perched high on his forehead.

Kristen shrugged. "I've had a lot on my mind today," she admitted.

"Really? Like what?"

Kristen was beginning to think she liked her brother better when he was self-absorbed. "Um...I dunno," she sighed again. "Just thinking of taking next semester off. Maybe."

Erik's jaw dropped. Rightfully so. She'd worked so hard to get accepted into this program. Not to mention she'd dreamed of becoming a marine biologist for as long as she could remember.

"Is Greene working you too much?" he asked.

"Yeah. Something like that." She was never particularly good at lying to her brother. But it wasn't like she was really lying. Just...withholding information for the time being. She had to tell Dane first.

Change that. First, she had to know for sure.

"O—kay." Judging by his tone, he obviously didn't believe her. "Hey, mind if I hang out here for a while?"

"Suit yourself," she said. "But I've got some things to do." Kristen hopped off the couch and grabbed her keys and wallet. She gave her brother one final wave as she headed out the door. Keeping this a secret was already proving much harder than she'd imagined.

Chapter Ten

BahamasAir Flight 223 departing Miami

Simon Greene boarded the plane in Miami with mixed feelings. Canceling a lecture was one thing. But he really shouldn't be leaving his research. Not now when he was on the verge of a major discovery.

Still...that many whales. This incident in the Bahamas could be another opportunity that earned him name recognition. And name recognition–especially on the eve of his scientific breakthrough–was always good.

Life sure hadn't turned out as Simon had originally planned, however. He attended Dartmouth University for his undergraduate degree with the intent to pursue pediatrics like his father. But after spending a summer taking a marine biology course at University of New Hampshire and Cornell University's jointly owned Shoals Marine Laboratory on Appledore Island off the coast of Maine, he dropped out of Dartmouth's ultra-competitive pre-med program.

Somewhere in the middle of a high-speed pursuit of fin whales–while most of his classmates hurled over the side of the whale watching boat as it tossed upon the churning waters of the Gulf of Maine–Simon had a change of heart. He pitied these majestic creatures, their immense tail flukes propelling them forward at top speed to escape the chasing boat. In their wake he observed only a trail of silky footprints: flattened patches of smooth water upon the ocean's surface from each thrust of their powerful flukes. Unable to catch these swift giants that were second only in size to the blue whale, the captain contacted other whale watching boats in the area, hoping someone had a lead on another pod of whales.

Eventually the captain's luck changed. The marine naturalist onboard sighted a pair of humpbacks a few hundred yards off the port side. Simon rushed to the railing, his heart skipping a beat as he spotted an adult humpback surfacing. Its characteristic puff of mist hung suspended like a bifurcated cloud above the darkened sea. The humpback's white pectoral fins–the longest of any whale–appeared as pale green, fifteen-foot patches, easily identifiable below the surface of the water. Soon the captain radioed in two more vessels that encircled the whales, confining them for better viewing opportunities. Each boat cut its engines to avoid scaring the mother and calf, while floating upon the waves to form a corral.

Simon dashed down to the lowest deck, leaning as far over the edge as possible to get a better glimpse of these majestic creatures. At that moment, the mother rolled onto one side, her enormous eye–the size of a large orange–catching his gaze. Simon froze, enraptured by the intelligence he saw within. A wave of compassion engulfed him, saddened by the whale's sudden loss of freedom, trapped as an object of entertainment for New England's summer tourists.

Clutching the handrail, he stared back, trying to imagine what other thoughts consumed this creature's mind. Did he detect fear inside her eyes? Fear for her personal safety or that of her calf? Did she know that some countries violated the International Whaling Commission's moratorium on commercial whaling and still illegally hunted their kind?

Or was it hope? Was she aware that the humpbacks' population had teetered on the brink of extinction, but slowly, amazingly, was coming back?

Or was it simple curiosity? Could it be that these humpbacks desired to understand more about us humans on the surface, the beings who pestered these placid mammals from the protection of our noisy vessels?

Before Simon had a chance to decide which thought weighed most heavily on the whale's conscious, the creature rotated back onto its belly, gave a few thrusts of its powerful tail flukes, and dove deep below the group of three ships bobbing on the surface like bath toys in an enormous tub. Soon after, the calf followed its mother, arcing its back as it dove. Just before disappearing into the depths of the sea, it raised its tail, exposing the fingerprint-like black and white markings on the underside of its flukes. Cameras rapidly clicked around Simon, capturing the last view of the sinking humpback. Then the captains started up their engines once more, setting off to search for a new pod of whales.

After they returned to the dock, Simon hiked up the steep slope of Appledore Island, his legs wobbly from spending hours shifting his weight to compensate for the pitch and yaw of the rolling sea. Just before reaching his temporary dormitory at the summit of the island, he turned. Gazing past the squawking gulls feeding their chicks, Simon looked out at the vast expanse of ocean stretching to the horizon. Inspired.

As he lay upon his cot that evening, listening to the distant sound of the crashing surf upon the rocky shore, he contemplated his future. Early the next morning, when the herring gulls squawked incessantly with the approaching dawn, Simon woke feeling energized and focused. He no longer pictured himself attending to coughing, snotty-nosed kids and their overanxious mothers. Instead, he envisioned himself spending the majority of his time out at sea, intending to gain a better understanding of these mysterious marine creatures. Although his original fascination lay with the enormous baleen whales, Simon soon became most intrigued with toothed whales: everything from communicating with other members of their pod to producing blasts of sound powerful enough to stun prey.

After Dartmouth, Simon Greene traveled to the Pacific Northwest to explore the dialects of the transient and resident pods of orcas dwelling along the east side of Vancouver Island for his graduate research and dissertation at the University of Washington. Then he moved to the Big Island of Hawaii for his post doc at the University of Hawaii-Hilo where he studied the spinner dolphins and pilot whales off the Kona coast. He'd spent the past two years as an associate professor at the Southern Florida State University investigating bottlenose dolphin communication and echolocation. He expected his current research project to generate the largest advances, however. And hopefully secure him a position as a tenured professor.

Using the optical and audio recording opportunities provided within the new telecommunications conversion to 7G, Simon hoped to bridge the gap between humans and whales. By adapting a set of eye DOTS to fit Allie, a 14-year-old bottlenose dolphin housed at the Miami Aquarium, Simon believed he would finally enable people–both researchers and civilians alike–to experience the underwater world as whales do…through sound.

Simon also hoped his research would aid the International Whaling Commission in retaining its ban against commercial fleets, despite mounting pressure from Japan, Iceland, and Norway to allow whaling practices to resume. These countries claimed that whale populations have increased sufficiently to allow annual harvesting. It wasn't like the ban prevented this. Illegal slaughters occurred anyway, regardless of the law. Plus hunting for "scientific purposes" was permitted–though whale meat could often be found in Japanese and Norwegian public marketplaces.

He knew his scientific data would protect these creatures–once whalers, scientists, and the general public better understood the actual intelligence of these social animals. Though his research would commence with eye and ear DOTS on bottlenose dolphins to enrich our comprehension of echolocation, the applications were vast. Simon imagined whale researchers all over the world making tremendous gains. In the Hawaiian Islands, scientists could finally unravel the mystery of humpback whale song. In the Pacific Northwest, they could decode orca dialects from resident and transient pods. In Patagonia, they could protect the severely threatened right whale populations. And along the coast of New Zealand, they could explore the deep-sea battles between the sperm whale and its favorite prey, the giant squid.

Of course, none of this would happen if he didn't get back to Miami before the National Conversion. He'd lose out on name recognition, funding, even his tenure track if someone else beat him to the discovery. And in the scientific world, you didn't dare finish second.

Chapter Eleven

The plane touched down at the quaint terminal on Nassau. Simon slung his backpack over one shoulder and squinted into the bright sun as he walked across the hot tarmac. He expected to find Roy Jackson at baggage claim like usual. Instead, Roy stepped out from under the shaded awning, meeting him with long strides across the blazing asphalt. Must be pretty urgent, Simon thought. Why else would the Transportation Security Administration give Roy clearance past the airport's X-ray screening stations?

Roy extended his hand to shake Simon's firmly. "Glad you could make it. The situation's gotten worse."

Simon raised his eyebrows. "How so?" He'd already mentioned the multiple strandings. How much worse could it possibly get?

Roy shot a worried glance at the tourists filing off the plane. "I'll explain in the car." He turned full circle and marched inside the terminal.

Roy Jackson had really changed since college. Even since the last time Simon had been out here a few months back. As always, Roy dressed in a white, long sleeved button down shirt and navy pants, though he never seemed to mind the heat. A patch of the seal of the Islands surrounded by a marlin and a pink flamingo adorned his right breast pocket. But this time Roy's face looked weary and gaunt; his normal jovial smile smothered by responsibility. His black curly hair cropped ultra-short was flecked with gray from mounting stress. Trouble at home? Simon wondered. Roy's shoulders slumped as he led Simon through the airport terminal.

Simon jammed his other arm through his backpack strap, barely able to keep Roy's pace as they sped down the florid carpeting. Past arrangements of bright orange and blue birds of paradise and scarlet anthuria in large vases. Past the quiet, deeply tanned tourists waiting to board their planes. Past the twitching eyes of those passengers using the current 6G Network technology to surf the Internet, send a text, or read an ebook while they waited. And past the mute kids who stared into space, engaged with a movie their parents had selected to guarantee acceptable behavior. Heck, parents even slapped pairs of ear DOTS on their infants. Piggybacking off their parents' mobile uplinks, babies napped to the melodies of Beethoven and Mozart.

Just wait until 7G came. They'd have so many more options. Instantaneous optical and audio recording. Dream uploads. And interspecies communication in the underwater world...provided he got back in time.

Preoccupied with the presumed benefits and applications of the new technology, Simon hadn't seemed to notice that not only had the DOTS taken on a babysitting role; they'd effectively eliminated personal conversation and interaction.

But before he had a chance to contemplate this issue further, he and Roy passed baggage claim and headed outside. A government-issued old Chevy sedan waited in the NO PARKING zone. Roy tipped the airport security personnel and unlocked the doors, tossing Simon's backpack into the trunk. A car like this would've been trashed a decade ago in the States for not complying with the Clean Air Bill, but out here, regulations were rarely enforced. How could they when there was no money to enforce them?

Simon closed his door and rolled down his window to dilute the smell of stale cigarette smoke. "You were saying?"

Roy turned the key in the ignition and shifted out of park. As he merged with traffic exiting the airport, he began, "The mother beaked whale didn't make it. Our local vets conducted a necropsy before her carcass rotted in the sun."

"And?"

"We're still waiting on pathology. But the overall inspection revealed nothing unusual. Except for hemorrhaging near her ears and melon."

Simon knew that in order to echolocate, toothed whales pushed air back and forth through an intricate series of sacs connected to their blowholes. Generating high frequency sounds similar to sonar, toothed whales project these sound waves out through an organ of fatty tissue called the melon located inside the forehead. The waves bounce off nearby objects and return as vibrations received by the whale's lower jaw. In turn, the vibrations are transmitted to the inner ear at the base of the jaw, then on to the brain for processing. Echolocation is vitally important amongst toothed whales and dolphins for communication between individual members of a pod, location of prey, and navigation in their underwater world.

Roy's news didn't sound good, but at least it confirmed Simon's suspicions. "So where is she now?" Simon asked.

"They dumped the body."

Simon frowned. Little was known about the rare, deep-diving beaked whales. He wished they hadn't towed the mother out to sea; he would've liked to save the skeleton. But Roy was more concerned with upholding the image of the

Islands than in conducting scientific research. And, of course, figuring out who is to blame. That's why he called in Simon.

"And the calf?"

"At a holding tank at the Atlantis Hotel. It's in fair condition and under continuous observation. We're hoping to release it in a few months," Roy said optimistically.

Doubtful, Simon thought. Beaked whales rarely survived that long in captivity. "What about the spinner dolphin?"

"Fortunately, we were able to save the spinner. Our rescuers set it on a stretcher and dragged it down the beach to the sea. It restranded once, but we managed to haul it out again. Thus far it hasn't been sighted again."

Simon shook his head. After the shock and stress of stranding twice, the spinner dolphin probably ended up dying at sea, its lifeless body sinking to rot on the ocean floor.

So what was the cause? Simon ran through a mental list of possibilities for the strandings. It was hurricane season, but he'd certainly know if a tropical storm had blown through the area. So that ruled out one possibility. "Any unusual fluxes in water temperature?"

Roy looked skeptical. It was the Caribbean after all.

"How about magnetic anomalies? Changing geography or fetch of the beach?" Simon asked. Roy shook his head.

Simon suspected as much. With so many different species involved — plus evidence of internal injury in the beaked whale — an unexpectedly loud noise was more likely the culprit. "What about offshore drilling? Or unusual ships in the area?"

"Now that you mention it, officials picked up a U.S. Navy submarine of undetermined class about thirty miles off the coast of Freeport on Grand Bahama Island shortly afterwards…" Roy's voice trailed off as he studied Simon incredulously. "You don't think the naval exercises have something to do with it, do you?"

"Actually, it might explain everything," Simon said grimly.

The extremely loud pulses of active sonar from a submarine might have attributed to the strandings and subsequent deaths. Sound travels further and five times faster underwater than through air, echoing off underwater objects and formations. For many years, scientists warned that loud sounds from naval exercises can cause marine mammals to change their natural behaviors, increase the animals' stress thereby leading to a decline in health, disrupt their communications with other members of the pod, and result in hearing damage. But he'd need more evidence to be certain.

"When can I see the pilot whales?"

"We're headed there first."

As Roy drove for miles down the road–past overgrown, faded pastel-colored shacks in various states of neglect–he and Simon fell silent, contemplating the fate of the whales.

With such a dismal future for these creatures, Simon felt compelled to break the ice. "So, how're the wife and kids?"

Roy shrugged. "Can't complain. And you?" He glanced at Simon meaningfully. "Find a potential 'Mrs.' yet?"

Simon shook his head and looked away. "Been too busy with work to even get out. With the upcoming conversion and all. I'm expecting this to be huge in understanding toothed whale communication."

Truth was, Simon's previous girlfriend griped about him becoming the classic workaholic, never committing to their relationship. That he spent more time with Allie than with her. Not that it mattered; bachelorhood suited him just fine. He didn't have anyone telling him what to do. At home, he was his own boss.

At least he kept telling himself that. It was as good an excuse as any to devote more time to his research.

Roy turned to the left, crossing the bridge linking the capital of Nassau and Paradise Island. Simon gazed out the window as they passed, noticing a few stress fractures forming in the concrete supports. In the U.S., the current administration funneled billions of taxpayer's dollars into defense to fuel its ongoing wars in the Middle East, while the nation's infrastructure had begun to fail: bridges breaking, dams bursting, levees rupturing. Much-needed repairs were delayed for lack of funding.

Here in the Caribbean, the U.S.'s recession had widespread effects as well. Declining rates of tourism left countries like the Bahamas–that relied on American dollars to fund their economy–in shambles. Everything was put on hold in hopes it would last until they had the money for repairs. The upgrade to 7G promised to jumpstart the economy, ending this prolonged recession once and for all. A gaggle of start-ups, including the rising Dreamscape, heralded a promising future by spending millions on advertising their new website designed to explore the fascinating human subconscious of the dream world. Though excited about the research applications, Simon expected his program with whale communication to prove profitable as well. Yet he had little time to consider these possibilities at the moment.

Paradise Island was anything but.

Simon remembered coming out here for spring break in college. While Roy had tried his luck in the casinos, Simon spent most of his time underwater, reveling in the pristine clear water, the tropical fish swimming about the reef, and the vast stretches of white sand.

Now it had transformed into a totally different scene.

On the beach, rescuers had roped off a wide area surrounding the stranded pilot whales. Despite the wretched smell, a growing throng of people had gathered to watch. Tourists and locals alike—women with braided hair in skimpy string bikinis and guys in Hawaiian print surf shorts with young children clinging to their thighs, dark-skinned women in floral dresses and men in worn T-shirts and jeans—looked on with mixed curiosity and fear. "Excuse me, please," Simon repeated as he squeezed his way through the packed crowd.

The once pleasant beach had become a nightmare of grisly proportions. Black pilot whales lay covered in assorted beach towels and blankets. A bucket brigade transported a steady stream of water to keep the whales cool and wet in the rising midday sun. Outside of their natural environment, whales easily sunburned and overheated; their thick blubber layer and dark hides essentially baked them from the inside.

After visually inspecting the survivors' pale gums and foamy green fecal samples—sure signs of shock—Simon began a necropsy for the few specimens that had perished on the beach, cutting three-centimeter square samples of major organs to send to pathology.

He wasn't certain which was worse: contending with the overwhelmingly putrid stench of roasting carcass here in the Caribbean's blinding sun, or completing this entire process in the cold, driving rain like he'd done in Cape Cod. At least he wouldn't end up in the emergency room like Barry Cohen who slipped off the back of the slick, rubbery skin of a beached right whale one summer at Woods Hole Oceanographic Institute in Massachusetts. Cape Code is infamous for confounding deep-sea whales with its changing geography, especially after a severe storm like the hurricane that had barreled up the coast a few days before. The endangered North Atlantic right whale was too large to move to the lab, so they completed the necropsy in full on sight — despite the rain and storm surge remaining from the passing storm. Working up by the blowhole, Barry had slipped, falling right onto the rescuer below, who–unfortunately for Barry–wielded a sharp knife. Barry ended up in the ER with 20 stitches in his thigh.

Stitches were the least of Simon's concerns at the moment. In fact, the sun was so merciless today, if he didn't complete his task soon, all evidence would be lost. Then he'd lack the necessary data that might link accountability of this accident to the U.S. Navy, leaving the Bahamians with the full expense of disposal, pathology reports, care of the infant beaked whale, and clean up costs. These people didn't have the resources to fund this project alone. Nor should they have to.

With dismay, Simon realized he should have brought his grad student, Kristen Weber, with him. Despite her inexperience in these matters, he could really use an extra hand right now.

Wiping the sweat from his brow, Simon set to work, endeavoring to slice through the thick blubber as readily as cutting tenderloin with a butter knife. Simon stifled a gag as he finally broke through the layer of blubber. Unfortunately, he still had the length of its abdomen to open–no easy feat when the whale stretched fifteen feet in length. He wiped the perspiration from his face, wishing he had something to repel the vile smell.

At least the stench had thinned the crowd whose curiosity was eventually overcome by the widespread odor of rot and decay. Hours passed while they worked on. And with the passing time, the tide rose to meet the beached whales once more.

Taking a break from the necropsies, Simon helped the rescuers push the surviving pilot whales out to sea. The remaining onlookers roared in jubilation. But Simon could only muster a forced smile. He knew the odds. Chances were slim for these rescued whales. Tomorrow, they'd probably wash ashore again.

This time, to die.

Chapter Twelve

Southern Florida State University off-campus housing

Kristen Weber perched on the edge of the toilet seat, her attention focused on the rising stream seeping up through the wand, leaving a pinkish trail. She'd read through the directions twice already, but still clutched them tightly in her hand while waiting for the appearance of a vertical line when the hormones in her urine reached the second window of the stick.

She was terrified someone would find out. So as a precaution, she'd paid extra to travel the light rail–Miami's latest effort to comply with U.S. Clean Air Bill and reduce traffic congestion–two towns past her normal grocery shopping stop, hoping she wouldn't bump into anyone she knew at the store. As it was, she felt like arrows in brilliant neon lights trained upon her, advertising UNMARRIED AND KNOCKED-UP to the cashier and every customer in the store. Not like they cared. She wasn't the first. Besides, most seemed preoccupied as their eyes darted back and forth, texting mundane messages to their spouses back home as to what items they should purchase for dinner tonight. Should I get the angel hair pasta or thin spaghetti? Roma or vine-ripened tomatoes? Kristen rolled her eyes. For crying out loud, make a decision on your own already!

Kristen had clandestinely searched out the pregnancy test section, draping her long blonde curls over the sides of her face and cramming her naked left hand into her front jeans pocket while she examined the different products. Their boxes pledged faster, more accurate results. Wouldn't you think with all of the recent technological advances, they could at least make a pregnancy test that yielded instantaneous results?

This was going to be the longest three minutes of her life.

There were probably a thousand things Kristen could've done to pass those three minutes, but all she could focus on was the lime green digital clock in the upper corner of her right periphery of the eye DOTS, its colon blinking with each passing second as she waited for the results to appear. What would Dane think now? Their relationship took a turn for the worst right before he left for his internship in D.C. His farewell kiss seemed forced, lacking passion. And their subsequent long-distance relationship had proven tenuous at best. Would this news improve his feelings toward her? Or was it the proverbial straw that broke the camel's back, enough for him to end things once and for all, leaving her to raise their child alone. She'd have to dump the kid in day care while she finished her doctorate. Or drop out of the program altogether — after how hard she'd worked to get accepted in the first place.

No, Kristen thought with fresh determination. She'd only resent her unborn baby for cutting short her dreams. She'd find a way to make it work. Even if she had to take a year off.

And her family? Her parents would certainly not condone this course of action. But would they support her? Erik, yes. He was always there for her when she needed him.

Though Kristen wasn't sure she was ready to tell him yet (or anyone else for that matter).

The timer hadn't gone off on her eye DOTS, but Kristen already knew the result. The second line appeared in bold magenta, almost mocking in its intensity.

Positive.

Dane couldn't possibly reject her now...not when she was carrying his child.

Could he?

Kristen instinctively lifted her shirt, slowly spinning from side to side as she studied her belly in the mirror. There was a very slight bulge, which could easily pass for bloating. She still had some time before she'd start to show.

Time to figure things out before the rumors started to fly.

Chapter Thirteen

Quarantine Room, U.S.S. Siren

Seaman Apprentice Alyssa Kensington lay on the thin mattress, staring up at the metallic ceiling. The past few hours proved a hazy recollection of painful memories–and a test of perseverance to resist clawing her itchy eyes.

Without her eye and ear DOTS, Alyssa's period of quarantine had quickly become unbearably dull. After scouring the room's concealed storage compartments, unable to find a single archaic paperback or magazine to peruse, she'd flopped on the bed, frustrated with her state of ennui. Why would anyone bother to stow printed books when they had a wealth of information — eBooks, movies, and music– instantly accessible through the DOTS' uplink with the Internet or the Siren's database?

And with the latest upgrade occurring tomorrow, information would arrive at an even faster speed, without the hassle of transporting the pocket-sized Mobile Uplink Digital Equipment around. The new MUDEs would be wafer thin, the size of her dog tags, and designed to be as inconspicuous as a gold charm worn around one's neck or wrist. Not only would the United States' telecommunications industry be at the pinnacle of the world with the new DOTS' recording capabilities, but the general populace would no longer need to physically carry anything in their pockets or purses. Credit card numbers, driver's licenses, and other personal forms of identification could easily be installed upon the new MUDEs, making the old handheld versions and any remaining cellular or Smartphones obsolete.

Granted, most people onboard the sub used the new devices almost constantly. Compulsive gamers somehow managed to multi-task, completing their assigned duties while interacting with other Siren personnel in battle games. Alyssa easily spotted them at the Mess Hall–the seamen whose fingers twitched sporadically, their eyes darting from side to side as they inhaled their food. Some of the new recruits were so obsessed with gaming that their eyes began to get the shakes: involuntary spasms even when they weren't using their eye DOTS. Alyssa couldn't look at them for long; she found their incessant twitching unnerving.

Of course Alyssa enjoyed her DOTS, too, having the opportunity to listen to her favorite songs and movies in stereo while she ate. Yet the convenience came with a price. Everyone else on board seemed so preoccupied in their virtual worlds that she rarely engaged in personal interaction with her colleagues over meals. It was almost as if the advanced technology actually distanced humans from one another, instead of bringing them closer together as was the original intent of mobile communication.

Alyssa avoided utilizing the equipment while on duty, however. Ever wary of the wrath of her superiors, she feared she wouldn't successfully complete her assigned duties if tempted by the wealth of resources and entertainment options available through the blink of an eye. On the virtual keyboard suspended in front of her face, she merely directed her attention toward a specific button to upload one of thousands of free movies or song choices from the sub's database. Or she could access her uploaded files of digital photos–a luxury when forbidden many personal items on board

Her DOTS also provided the flexibility of "visiting" the nearby Caribbean Islands, even though she remained below the surface. Using their current latitude and longitude coordinates, Alyssa virtually toured nearby islands on the sub's database, pretending she lounged on white sandy beaches or shopped for souvenirs in the local markets. She'd read up on the island's culture and history, particularly enjoying the old pirate tales from each port.

Of course it wasn't the same as a vacation, missing out on the local flavor and scents, the fresh breeze rustling her hair, the sun beating down on her face, and lounging on the beach to work on her tan...but it was a huge improvement from the monotonous scenery she had on board.

Though the monotonous scenery seemed preferable to her current situation.

Guilt consumed Alyssa for the probable epidemic she created. (How long would it be before Rosemary and the others began to develop symptoms of conjunctivitis?) And for the untimely deaths of those stranded whales and dolphins, possibly linked to her actions aboard the U.S.S. Siren. Of course, she wasn't the only one responsible–she was following orders, after all. But Alyssa had actually pushed the button, thereby initiating the active sonar test. If she hadn't done so, those defenseless animals would probably still be alive.

Shortly after the test, the Siren had risen to periscope depth to resume communications with their satellite link and report the results to the Naval Research Officials, Alyssa suspected. Whatever the reason, the submariners found themselves with unexpected access to the World Wide Web before the Siren dove deep again. A source of much excitement, word quickly spread throughout the Mess Hall. After checking her email and sending a few texts, Alyssa surfed the net while she ate, eager for more information on the nearby Caribbean ports of call.

That's when she'd stumbled across several articles and blogs posted by local scientists and marine mammal rescuers following the Siren's test. Two beaked whales, eleven pilot whales, and a spinner dolphin all reportedly stranded onshore in the Bahamas. Apparently, the scientists found the whales had no prior health problems. The reports did mention, however, that the whales were bleeding from their ears and brain, possibly linked to intense sound waves like those generated during active sonar tests.

Alyssa gasped, making the connection. Her sub had been near the Bahamas at the time of their test. The reports were talking about the Siren.

She was a murderer.

Granted, the Siren's commanding officers and the XO had reassured her that the data collected during these tests would save thousands of submariners in the future. If the Navy were to implement this advanced prototype of active sonar for the entire Hydra class of submarines, they would gain the enhanced ability to scan the ocean floor and identify enemy subs at a much greater range. What did it matter if a few animals died in the process of this new discovery? Their deaths were not necessarily triggered by the test. All over the world, whales beach themselves for a variety of reasons: illness, changing shoreline contours, storms...

Only this time Alyssa doubted her chain of command.

Her mind reeled as she relived intense feelings of remorse. She tried to close her eyes, but couldn't block out the images of the eleven dead pilot whales littering the sandy beach.

All because of her.

"I honestly had no idea," Alyssa whispered, attempting to reassure herself. "I was just following orders." But her voice was weak. Unconvincing.

Besides, what action would she take during their upcoming test scheduled for next week? Would she be able to conduct another active sonar test, now that she knew the possibility of a repeated outcome? Just thinking about the loud ping resonating through her eardrums sent shivers down her spine.

A sudden knock on the door jarred her from another pity session. Who could possibly be coming to see her? She didn't think she was permitted any visitors.

Alyssa scrambled off the end of the mattress to open the door, but found no one there. Only a tray covered in aluminum foil. She snatched her lunch and placed it on the bed, not before realizing her ravenous hunger until she smelled the intoxicating scent of a greasy cheeseburger and fries. Peeling the wrapper, she leaned closely, closing her eyes as she relished the first bite.

Usually Alyssa loved burger days; often lingering a few minutes after finishing her meal to savor the smell of grease from the deep fryer and cheeseburgers off the grill. Closing her eyes, she'd pretend she was in her backyard in central Virginia instead. While her mom grilled corn on the cob and burgers, Alyssa would set the table, then immerse herself in a book until dinner was served. Her golden retriever, Tucker, lounged under the patio table by her feet, patiently awaiting his traditional handout at the end of the meal.

As the sun dropped below the horizon, its last rays tickled the undersides of the clouds, bathing them in muted shades of pink and peach blossoms. Alyssa would lean back in an Adirondack chair on her wrap-around porch, enchanted with the bright oranges and reds that followed, like tongues of wildfires dancing across the sky.

As the sunset faded into darkness, pinpricks of starlight became visible above the shadowed, rolling peaks of the Blue Ridge Mountains. Tiny gleams of fireflies soon sparkled across her dusky backyard, like dozens of miniature candles repeatedly lit, then extinguished. Their abdomens flashed brightly as each searched for a mate.

When she was younger, she'd run barefoot across the thick grass with Tucker at her heels, seeing how many lightning bugs she could catch inside a Dixie cup. Covering the top with her hand, she'd create a homemade paper lantern, emanating a warm glow as the shroud of nightfall descended upon the valley.

Alyssa took another bite of her burger, inhaling deeply to block out the stale smell of the recycled air, desperate for her old life. She hadn't predicted how much she'd miss the hint of pine and oak as the wind rustled through the forest. The delectable fragrances of honeysuckle and wildflower sweetly carried on the breeze. Even the dank smell of wet dog as Tucker emerged from his dip in the creek, spraying her when he shook off.

Finishing her meal, she stacked her tray upon the sink and laid down again, hoping that with a satiated stomach, sleep would find her.

It never did.

Chapter Fourteen

Restless and achy from lack of movement, Alyssa squirmed on the mattress, unable to find a comfortable position.

Squeezing her eyes shut, she tried to block out the agonizing memories of her deadly sonar test, her contagious condition, her forbidden love. Nevertheless, her thoughts inadvertently turned toward the first time she laid eyes on Justin. Alyssa knew it was foolish to allow her heart to prevail over logic and reason, yet she felt powerless to change her fate.

They set sail on one of those typical southern Triple-H days: hot, hazy, and humid. Wearing her smoke gray and blue camouflage service uniform and matching beret, Alyssa felt professional, ready to tackle any challenge she'd confront while on duty. She carried only a small drawstring backpack of the few personal effects she was permitted onboard. But after a few minutes of standing outside in the blistering sun with the rest of her future crewmates, Alyssa was dripping. Her shirt clung to the thin layer of perspiration across her back and under her armpits. Beads of sweat trickled down her neck and pooled inside her collar.

"I've got a funny feeling about this," Linda Kensington whispered, as if disclosing a vital secret. Tears welled up in the corners of her eyes as she squeezed Alyssa's hand.

Though Alyssa was glad she had someone to see her off, in a way she wished it were someone less embarrassing than her mother. But since she broke up with Steve and Ellen had to work, she didn't have other options. Alyssa shifted uncomfortably on her feet, thinking of something to say to mollify Linda. At least the seamen closest to her seemed too preoccupied to overhear their conversation.

"Why's that?" Alyssa replied distractedly as she glanced around the platform, watching the other submariners bid farewell to loved ones. Young infants squirming in the arms of their parents. Couples clinging to each other, professing their I-love-yous. Luckily, they could converse with their families back home through the DOTS—at least until the Siren sank below periscope depth. How did the World War I era navy crews manage, Alyssa wondered, when their sole communications occurred by mail whenever they reached port?

Her mom sighed deeply, as if releasing a huge weight from her shoulders. "Honey, I'm really worried about you."

"Worried?" Alyssa snorted, running her fingers through her short brown hair. She still hadn't adjusted to its new length. "Mom, I told you before that we're not going to be in danger." After all, the U.S.S. Siren was sailing off to conduct a series of tests for a highly advanced and more powerful prototype active sonar system–not to engage in warfare.

Linda's voice cracked as the tears spilled over, "I feel like I'm never going to see you again."

Alyssa rolled her eyes. "Oh, Mom. Please!" She patted Linda's back in reassurance, just as she'd done all those years after Dad died. Tucker would have to provide adequate company for her mother until Alyssa returned on leave. "I'll be back in a few months. I promise."

Granted, there were risks involved on the Siren: fighting fires, fixing leaks, and contending with the intense pressure of the surrounding water that forever bore down upon the double-layered hull of the ship. But at least she didn't fear sinking by an enemy sub or accidentally falling overboard like if she were on an aircraft carrier.

No need to disclose such information, Alyssa figured; it would only augment her mother's worry. Besides, Alyssa was certain that she would be fine. Linda wouldn't be decorating the trees in their front yard with yellow ribbons again.

Nevertheless, Linda clung to Alyssa madly, her voice choked with tears.

Alyssa glanced over at the top of the sub sitting above the surface, its tear-dropped black hull perfect for hiding underwater. Which was exactly what Alyssa wished to do right now: hide. She couldn't wait to begin the boarding process.

It was then that she spotted him standing alone, patiently waiting.

He lifted his face toward the sun, as if savoring the last few moments of daylight for sustenance during the next six months underwater. Despite the discomfort Alyssa felt in this oppressive heat, sandwiched between couples with lips locked in parting, he seemed perfectly at ease. Alyssa studied the seaman, his military buzz cut obscured by his beret, his dark complexion shiny in the baking sun. Just like her, he wore the Stars and Stripes over his left shoulder. The sun caught one of decorations, making his golden dolphin fish pin glitter brightly. An officer. Alyssa glanced down at her own submariner insignia, embroidered in silk, like the other enlisted men. She wouldn't earn this prestigious award until she made officer herself.

Alyssa never believed in love at first sight. But something about the officer held her enraptured. Maybe it was the confidence he emanated. Or his muscular chest, angled cheekbones, and warm, deep eyes. But whatever the reason, Alyssa couldn't take her eyes off him. Smothered in her mother's embrace, she'd stopped listening to her mom's growing list of concerns of Alyssa's impending peril.

Squinting, Alyssa tried to perceive the name centered above the officer's right breast pocket. She could only make out an H, I, and D before he caught her glance, smiling in an amused way. Alyssa's face flushed hot as she diverted her eyes. She knew from basic training that officers never mingled with her class. The consequences were too severe.

Redirecting her attention to her mother, she finished her goodbye, then slung her backpack over her shoulder and stepped into line. And kept her eyes on her feet.

Alyssa waved to Linda from the gangplank, then found a spot topside, away from the railing where those who desperately wanted one last opportunity to say farewell vied for position. Setting her backpack on her lap, she tried to remain still and forget about the officer in the muggy air as perspiration poured down her cheeks. Guided by a pair of tugboats, the sub finally pushed away from the dock and out toward the sea. The breeze felt hot against Alyssa's cheeks, but at least the air was moving to dry the sweat from her face.

A few minutes out, the submariners shuffled into line to descend below. Alyssa rose and slipped her backpack over her shoulders as she walked unsteadily across the 585-foot long, 45-foot wide black hull of the sub.

At the top of the ladder, Alyssa lingered. She suddenly realized the need for a memory to sustain her during the long months underwater. Scanning the horizon, her eyes landed on the solitary officer who'd smiled at her, stationed up on the Bridge of the sub's Sail. Not good, Alyssa, she scolded herself. Try something else. But her descent was long overdue; another seaman already waited his turn. Inhaling one last breath of the briny air, Alyssa sighed as she climbed down the ladder into the bowels of the metal beast.

After dropping off her bag at her assigned rack in the Torpedo Bay at the bow of the ship and changing into her navy blue work gear, Alyssa greeted her berthmate, Rosemary DeLa Cruz, with a brief handshake. Unlike Alyssa with her hair cut short, Rosemary wore her thick black hair up in a bun. Then they stowed their dress uniforms flat under the mattress, one on top of the other. Little did Alyssa realize this was one of the few exchanges the two of them would share for the duration of their tour.

As Alyssa navigated her way through the narrow corridors, allowing higher-ranking officers and crewman to pass by turning her back against the wall, she bumped into Carly Zapelli, one of her friends from basic training. Though assigned different shifts, the thought of a familiar face on board warmed Alyssa. She smiled the whole length of the corridor and down to the Command and Control Room. But when she reached her station, her smile quickly faded.

Not him again. Ducking past the group of officers milling near her station discussing the success of their initial descent, she immediately spotted the officer from the Bridge, despite the periwinkle blue background lighting that distorted the color of everyone's skin tones. Though she told herself not to look, she couldn't resist. Well, at least now she could make out his entire name: HIDALGO. Officer Hidalgo, she reminded herself.

While manning her station to familiarize herself with the sonar controls, Alyssa couldn't help but catch bits of the officers' conversation. She should've turned on her ear DOTS to block out the noise, yet curiosity overcame her. Apparently before the dive, they'd spotted dolphins. Unconsciously, Alyssa craned her neck, listening to Dive Officer Hidalgo describe the pod of bottlenose that rode the surf of the bow.

She closed her hazel eyes, imagining herself standing up on the Bridge, too. The ocean breeze rustled her bobbed hair as she watched the dolphins frolic in the submarine's generated waves while it plowed through the seas. Their arced silver backs glistened in the sun as they leapt from the water, one after another. A dreamy expression passed over her face as she opened her eyes, eager to hear more. Only she realized Officer Hidalgo had caught her staring at him. Again. He flashed her a quick grin, displaying all of his white teeth. Alyssa's face turned red as she wheeled back to her computer monitor, forcing herself to focus on the task at hand. "How could I be so stupid?" she muttered to herself. But it wasn't really her fault.

She couldn't help that he looked so amazing in his dress uniform.

Though she knew, deep down, she should demonstrate more restraint. Her future–and his–depended on it.

Chapter Fifteen

"Stop it, Alyssa!" she screamed, drowning her voice in her pillow. She had driven herself crazy reliving their first encounter. Resisting the overwhelming urge to rub her eyes, she sat up in bed again, stretching her stiff, achy joints. It must be that time again. Alyssa tilted her head back, letting the soothing liquid coat her irritated eyes. Placing the drops in her pocket, she blinked, then eased back onto her pillow, keeping her eyes closed.

Remembering…

"S.A. Kensington? Is that you?"

Alyssa blushed as she noticed Officer Hidalgo leaning against the Mess Hall door. Her heart leapt up her throat.

"What are you doing here?" he asked.

In a feeble attempt at nonchalance, she gestured toward the screen.

Justin Hidalgo turned, instantly grimacing at the near blinding movie screen. Quickly glancing to the side, he switched off the night mode on his eye DOTS. His grimace fading, he pulled out the chair next to Alyssa and settled down. "Right. I forgot all about the email. The Skipper's into nostalgia, I guess. Didn't know anyone actually came to these things."

"They don't," she snipped. Why would anyone attend these movie nights when they had full access to a vast wealth of movie titles at any time of the day? Officer Hidalgo must think she was the biggest loser on the ship.

"Is it any good?"

"Not really," she responded in a flat tone.

Hidalgo's voice softened. "Everything okay?"

She shrugged and crossed her arms, returning her attention to the movie. She shouldn't be here with him. Just speaking to him alone was a recipe for disaster.

Nevertheless, she spent the next ten minutes berating herself for acting so irritated. Just great. Her first attempt at normal conversation in the past few weeks and she blows it with her sour mood. From the corner of her eye, she peeked at his chair, convinced he was mad at her. Then again, he was so quiet, maybe he'd left altogether. But not only was his chair occupied; he appeared spellbound as he intently watched the film.

She cocked one eyebrow skeptically. "Officer Hidalgo? Can I ask you a question?"

"Sure." His eyes never left the screen.

"Do you like this movie?"

"Nope." A wide grin spread over his face. "Mostly, I was trying to figure out how you've managed to endure such a piece of crap this long."

Alyssa bent over double, a full-bellied roar. "It's been a test of my perseverance, that's for sure."

"I'll bet." He turned toward Alyssa, his face growing serious. "Can I ask you a question?"

Alyssa's eyes opened wide. She had no idea where this was leading. Had he picked up on her crush, possibly noticing her staring at him at the boarding dock? Or one of those other times she'd passed him in the Command and Control Room, her eyes lingering a bit too long on his visage? This was not going to be good.

"Um, okay," she replied tentatively. "Go ahead."

"Do you remember the day we set sail?"

Of course she did. Alyssa gulped. Oh God, Oh God. He knows! Why did I have to be so obvious? she fretted.

"Why-?" Hidalgo paused momentarily, as if searching for the appropriate words. Finding his voice again, he continued, "Why did you seem so interested in my story from the Bridge?"

A wave of relief spread over her face. Perhaps her feelings were not as apparent as she had assumed. "I'm sorry, Officer Hidalgo, I didn't mean-"

"It's just us here," he interrupted. "You can call me Justin."

Us. The mere concept of him considering them an entity warmed Alyssa from the inside, like the rosy glow of a campfire when she'd roast marshmallows on cool summer nights. She took a deep breath before apologizing, "I didn't mean to eavesdrop. I just wished I could have been up there on the Bridge, too, watching the dolphins leap from the water." (She purposefully omitted the part about being with him.) "It must have been pretty amazing."

Justin leaned back in his chair, recalling the event. "Yeah. It was."

Alyssa glanced at him again, a dreamy look glazing over his eyes. How many times had she longed for a moment to personally converse with someone? To break away from the daily routine of sub life? Now here she was-ironically with the object of her infatuation-and at a loss for words. Her stomach began to knot, thinking of the risk involved and what would happen if they were caught. She shouldn't be fraternizing with an officer. It could ruin him.

She really should get out of here. Mustering her resolve, she stood to go.

"You're leaving already?" Justin asked, placing his hand on her arm to stop her. She looked down at his hand. Touching her. His warmth penetrated her skin. Alyssa froze, speechless.

"It just seems like most people are too busy to talk these days," Justin explained. "I can't remember the last time I got a chance to just sit around and shoot the breeze with anyone."

Alyssa blinked. She couldn't believe what she was hearing. Against her better judgment, she sank back into her chair.

"You probably don't know how it is, but sometimes I feel like I just want a break from the constant barrage of information. Like I could go back to when I was a kid and would sit for hours under a blanket on a cold, rainy day, just reading a good book. You know...a real book. Holding it in your hands. Flipping the pages. The smell of the paper."

Alyssa's jaw dropped.

Justin noticed her reaction and stopped, frowning. "I know. I must sound like an idiot. I mean, really? Who'd trade immediate access to unlimited knowledge for a little thing like a book? It's stupid of me to even bring it up."

"I don't think it's stupid." She wished she could place her hand on top of his to comfort him, but refrained from the breach in rank. Instead, she confessed, "I feel that way sometimes, too."

He glanced up, his dark eyes locking with hers. "If it were anyone else, I'd say you were just trying to make me feel better. But for some reason...I actually believe you."

Alyssa spent the remaining hour of the movie doing something she had only dreamed of for so long, actually talking face to face with someone. And not just anyone, but Justin. His smile was infectious, his voice velvety, his eyes sympathetic and understanding. She felt drawn to him, confiding in him feelings she had not verbalized since they'd dove below the surface. They discussed their friends, families back home, and essentially any topic dealing with life topside. Though he had only just graduated from the Academy, he was made a dive officer with his stellar performance on the Navy's rigorous testing. He wasn't that much older than Alyssa. And he wasn't married. So what was holding her back?

Besides, he must feel something too; why else would he jeopardize him career with a secret relationship? Regardless of how her superiors would judge her, she knew this was inevitable. She and Justin had so much in common. Almost like they were meant to be together, whatever the cost. Alyssa could worry later about the repercussions should someone become privy to their budding relationship.

Then the movie ended. The screen went black. Justin slid to the edge of his chair. His face only inches from hers, his breath brushed against her lips. She didn't pull away.

Even though she knew she should've.

The anticipation of this single kiss intensified her feelings for him. Purposefully disregarding all of her previous reservations, Alyssa leaned closer, her mouth nearly touching his. Her heart thudded loudly inside her chest as their lips met, instinctively entwining. Her hands sought his body, drawing him near. His fingers traced her spine, making her shiver with pleasure.

Her desires these last few months finally gratified, Alyssa kissed him softly at first, then with escalating intensity. His fingers knotted in her hair as his lips kept pace with hers. Was he also starved for physical contact these long months aboard the sub?

Impossibly wonderful, Alyssa wished this moment could last forever, content at last in his arms. Inside, Alyssa stirred in longing, as if possessing Eve's burning desire for that proverbial forbidden fruit from the biblical dawn of humanity.

Suddenly, red lights flashed throughout the Mess Hall, accompanied by a blaring alarm. The siren's strident wail pierced the silence, annihilating the calm like the thunderous crash heard seconds before a lightning bolt splits the sky, bringing an end to an otherwise insufferably hot and muggy mid-summer night.

Alyssa jerked upright, instantly pushing away from Justin's embrace. Her initial reaction was one of shock, assuming they'd been caught. Inside her throat, her pulse throbbed wildly. With wild eyes darting around the room, she gratefully noticed they were still alone. "What is it?" she asked between erratic breaths, searching for an explanation to the abrupt end of this much-awaited romantic interlude.

Justin appeared equally stunned. Yet his expression quickly changed, his face radiating calm in the face of a storm as he assessed the situation. "I've gotta go. Probably a leak or something," he explained as he smoothed out his work uniform, his dark eyes sincere. Did she also detect a hint of regret? A glimpse of longing as he scooted off his chair and headed for the door? It was hard to say for sure.

Alyssa remained rooted to her chair, speechless. Her heart thumped outside of her chest, as if she'd just been jolted back to reality. Of course this emergency hadn't been planned, but it seemed far too coincidental to not perceive it as a warning. A last chance for Justin to change his mind before he made a mistake that could threaten his entire military career.

Alyssa bit her lip, controlling her emotions. What did she expect? That he wouldn't take the proffered way out?

If their places were reversed, she certainly would've done the same.

Before ducking out the door, Justin glanced back at Alyssa, a small grin upon his face. "I'll catch up with you later, 'kay?"

Alyssa nodded expectantly, watching him leave.

But later never came.

Chapter Sixteen

Easton Hall Dormitory, Southern Florida State University

PICK UP, ERIK!

"As if," Erik Weber muttered to himself, ignoring the flashing message from Rachael in his eye DOTS. It wasn't like he'd replied to any of her previous messages, so why start now? Besides, what could he possibly say? Hey, I saw you hugging another guy today. Erik's face flushed as he relived the memory. He'd never really thought of himself as the jealous type...until now.

Her message came again, this time in bright red. WE NEED TO TALK.

Erik's heart sank to the bottom of his chest like a cannon ball. Nothing good ever came from those four little words. So this was it, huh? She wanted to break up. It wasn't like it should come as a total shock to Erik. He knew the hazards of dating someone in your own dorm—he'd witnessed the awkward break-ups in the past. The discomfort of bringing home another girl and bumping into your ex. Only he never thought it would happen to him.

He'd run into Rachael Gallagher on moving day this year. Literally. Arms laden with boxes, he'd pushed open the doors and didn't see her small frame over the top. Knocked her flat on her butt. He'd immediately dropped his stuff and apologized, offering her a hand. When he pulled her to her feet, her eyes met his. Bright, bold blue, yet distant. Irritated.

Erik stammered like an idiot, unable to form a complete sentence...and unable to release his grasp. She finally wrenched her hand free and tramped down the hall. For weeks, she successfully ignored him whenever they passed. He couldn't say he blamed the girl, after flattening her and all. But her avoidance only made him want her more. A challenge he felt destined to overcome.

Then one Saturday night, he bumped into her at a Sigma Delt party. She was wasted and couldn't stop talking to him. Or anyone for that matter. Nor could she remember where her friends had gone. So Erik volunteered to walk her home. And ended up carrying her back to their dorm where she passed out on her bed.

The next day, she knocked on his door to apologize. Naturally, he blew it off. No one in his right mind would've left her there alone. But her attitude toward him had changed. She started talking to him in passing at their dorm. Joined him and his roommate, Lucas, for dinner in the dining hall. She'd walk to class with the two of them. Then with Erik alone.

Sometimes he and Rachael would skip class to meet back in the dorm when they knew their roommates were gone. Erik loved being close to her: touching her, hearing her teasing laugh, feeling the glow of her radiant eyes.

All gone now.

Wistful, Erik remembered those days when they were first getting to know everything about each other. The late nights in the common room talking when they should've been studying…and kissing long after the others had gone to bed.

Trying to ignore her the last twenty-four hours had been more than he could bear.

Face it, Erik. She was cheating on you. Still, he couldn't believe it. That was something he wouldn't've put past a few of his old girlfriends. But not Rachael.

PLEASE, ERIK. PICK UP!

Furious, Erik opened his eyes wide and fished out his eye DOTS, dropping them in an old contact lens case. He peeled off the ear DOTS, too, and took his MUDE out of his jeans' pocket, tossing them onto the desk in his room.

He needed some space. Someplace to get away from her constant messages. He certainly couldn't face her now—and hear her say it was over.

Instead, he needed to go somewhere she wouldn't find him. A place she'd never expect him of all people to be. Not on a Friday night…

The library.

Chapter Seventeen

Erik Weber walked up the Ross Library steps, feeling like a nerd. Who else would choose to come here over the parties on Frat Row?

As he entered, he nodded to the library clerk with a bad case of acne and a mop of thick, black hair working behind the front desk. The kid barely paid Erik any attention in return. With eyes skittering back and forth, he was probably preoccupied with some online video game on his DOTS. Speaking of which, why didn't Erik bother leaving his in? At least he could've streamed a movie or two to pass the time. Then again, Rachael's frequent texts would've undoubtedly popped up. "I want to explain," she'd claimed.

But there was nothing to explain. He'd caught her with another guy.

End of story.

And here he thought she was different from the other girls he'd dated in the past. Someone he could trust. The One even.

Until she broke his heart.

Kristen was right. Love sucks.

Erik headed through the doorway leading to the common study room, a large space with wooden cubbies along the perimeter and a sea of comfortable upholstered chairs in the center. On a typical afternoon, he remembered this place being swamped. But tonight...not so much. Big surprise there.

Erik's eyes scanned the room as he settled into a soft chair in the middle. Though the actual need for libraries had long since faded as e-libraries allowed patrons to download any eBook for free, the edifice itself still stood as a gathering place for students requiring a quiet place to study. The largely unused stacks of resources materials remained filled with antiquated dead-tree-books for lack of a better place to store them.

Tonight, the quiet of the common room rivaled that of the stacks. Two kids nestled at corner desks worked on problem sets–probably for some killer class like Orgo or Diff-E.Q. A third occupied a desk by the window, taking notes from his hardcover text. He obviously had one of the few professors on campus that still required students to purchase printed books.

Freshman year, Erik used to arrive here right after lunch to snatch one of the prized comfy chairs. And if he was lucky, he'd snag two and push them together like a boat–perfect for stretching out for an afternoon nap under the illusion of studying. He never failed to find at least one kid snoring, a bit of spittle oozing out of the corner of his mouth. Occasionally (Erik was ashamed to admit), it was him.

Though Erik hadn't been here in ages. Not since Rachael Gallagher came along.

Rachael. Maybe he should go and find her like Kristen'd suggested, Erik mused.

But what if she was already out with that guy? Erik wasn't the confrontational type. Especially not when he was so outmatched. Heck, Erik was athletic, too–at least before his parents signed him up for the full meal plan. He'd made the Varsity Baseball team at Fountainbleau High School three years in a row. But Varsity and Division 1 were two different stories. And that guy was definitely D-1 material. Lucas was right: Erik was out of his league.

Besides, being up all last night dwelling on Rachael certainly didn't help his situation. Erik needed to be fresh. So he wouldn't say something he'd later regret.

Erik's eyelids sagged, heavy with sleep. Promising himself he'd find her first thing tomorrow, he pulled a second chair over to prop up his feet. He only needed a little nap to pass the time before she headed out for the evening. Then he could go back to the dorm without the risk of bumping into her. And in the morning, things would be different. He'd look for her right after breakfast. No, he corrected himself, before. Go down and knock on her door. Somehow find a way to win her back.

Erik slid down into the chair, leaning his head against the soft armrest. He'd even admit that he loved her. Because now, faced with the prospect of losing her, he realized that he did.

Tomorrow, Erik thought. A small grin crept across his face as he drifted to sleep.

Chapter Eighteen

The Kensington home, Madison, Virginia

Steve Summers parked his silver Ford Focus across the street from a white Colonial with black shutters and a wrap-around porch. He hadn't been here since graduation and wasn't sure if he was even welcome after Alyssa made it plain she wanted nothing to do with him. Yet she was off at sea, and utterly incapable of protesting his unexpected arrival.

He shut off the ignition and took a deep breath. Her mother'd been alone all these months…and always had a soft spot for Steve. She wouldn't refuse his meager request. And even if she did, at least he never mentioned to anyone he planned to swing by Alyssa's house before picking Ellen up for dinner. Nothing good could possibly come of Ellen discovering he still had feelings for his ex.

Steve climbed out of the car, stuffed his keys into his jeans' pocket, and slammed the door shut. His palms felt cold and clammy, so he jammed them into his pockets next to the keys.

Just get this over with, he told himself with a sigh. Glancing over his shoulder in each direction, he crossed the street with a few long strides, then continued up the faded black-top driveway, stubby weeds poking out through its cracked surface.

Either she'll tell you or she won't, he reminded himself, but you'll never know for sure unless you ask. Right?

Still, Steve's stomach flipped upside-down as he neared Alyssa's door. He hoped he wasn't making a huge mistake, risking everything with Ellen–as tenuous as it might seem at times–for the glimmer of hope of regaining Alyssa's love.

Preoccupied in his thoughts, Steve failed to notice Alyssa's golden retriever, Tucker, bounding across the yard until he almost bumped into Steve. "Hey, buddy! How've you been?" Steve said, bending over to give Tucker a thorough scratch behind the ears. Tucker wagged his tail, thwacking Steve's leg on each pass.

The front door creaked open. An older version of Alyssa emerged onto the porch. Linda Kensington's short brown hair grayed at the roots, her face creased with concealed worry. As she dried her hands on a dishtowel, she called, "Tucker! Get back here!"

Steve raised his head and gave a small wave, "Hi, Mrs. K."

Linda squinted, her face suddenly brightening. "Steve? Is that you?"

He nodded while Tucker panted and slobbered over his outstretched hand. "He doesn't bark like he used to. Maybe he doesn't hate me coming around anymore," Steve said with a nervous smile.

"He never hated you coming here," Linda replied, her grin widening as she dropped the dishtowel on an Adirondack chair and made her way down the porch steps and across the yard. "It's his DOTS. I got so tired of how loud he got every time we had a visitor, that I thought I'd give them a try. That Bark Control's made a huge difference."

"I bet." Steve patted Tucker's head affectionately. He was like a totally different dog, as if someone turned his volume down to mute.

"But Steve! I can't believe you're here. It's so good to see you again!" she added as she neared, sweeping him into a fast hug. When Linda pulled away, her eyes glistened with tears, as if desperately clinging to every past memory of her only child. "So how are you? How is school?" she gushed. "You look great. You're so tan! Did you go somewhere?"

Steve shrugged, managing a faint smile while guilt weighed heavy upon his heart. At least she didn't ask how Ellen was doing. Maybe she didn't know.

Steve shifted on his feet, eager to change the subject, "I just thought I'd stop by. See if you've heard from Alyssa lately." The last thing he needed was to have Ellen wonder why he's late in picking her up.

Linda sighed, a wistful look in her eyes as she folded her arms over her chest. "You know how it goes. She's only allowed communication when they're near the surface. But I was hoping to get in touch with her tonight. I thought her sub might resume contact…with the Conversion and all."

Steve's face grew hopeful. "Tonight?" he echoed. That's so much better than he ever anticipated. Almost like instant gratification. Either Alyssa'll speak to him now or be done with him once and for all. He wasn't sure how he'd handle the second possibility, but perhaps it would never amount to that. And if it did, at least he never dumped Ellen. He couldn't stand being alone like Alyssa' mom. All those years and she never remarried. Sure, the emotional signs of strain were there, but what about satiating physical urges? How anyone could survive that long was impossible for him to fathom.

"Do you think Alyssa would have time to speak to me, too?" Steve wondered, hoping he didn't sound too desperate.

"I don't see why not. Why don't you grab a Coke from the fridge while I try to get a hold of her?" Linda's eyes lost his; suddenly flitting back and forth as she optically typed a message to her daughter.

Phew, Steve thought as he headed toward the house. That went easier than he'd expected...so far, at least. But before Steve reached the front door, he heard a chilling howl of pain. Spinning toward its source, he saw Tucker rolling on the ground, his paws frantically batting at his floppy ears.

"Oh, my God!" Linda shrieked as she knelt beside her dog. "Tucker? What's wrong?"

The howling persisted. Steve dashed back to help when an intense ringing pierced his ears. He heard Linda shriek again before clamping his hands over his eardrums. Dizzy from the unbearable sound, he fell to his knees. His eyes hammered inside his skull, pulsing wildly as if threatening to burst. What's wrong with me? Steve squeezed his head tighter to alleviate the pain, trickles of blood moistening his palms. Impossible to concentrate on anything besides the agony he faced, all external noise essentially disappeared, drowning out Tucker's dreadful wails and Linda's high-pitched screams.

Ellen would be pissed if he ditched her for dinner. Even more so if she found him here at Alyssa's house. But that concern rapidly lost importance. Unable to rise to his feet, he tumbled forward onto his belly, collapsing in a prone position against the driveway.

For a split moment, he looked up from his spot, noticing Tucker's body had grown quiet. Linda lay still beside him, her arm draped over his motionless form.

They're dead? he wondered, his heart gripped in fear. Impossible–they were fine just a minute ago!

But regardless of what caused their demise, Steve knew Alyssa would never forgive him for this. Not in a million years.

If he even saw her again.

Steve felt his willpower to endure this kind of agony quickly slip through his grasp. He struggled against the pain, wondering what he ever did to deserve this type of torture.

Before he could speculate an answer, something in his brain felt like it exploded. His consciousness faded into oblivion as blood pooled around Steve's face and ears, staining the weathered driveway in a deep red patch.

Chapter Nineteen

Coombs Science Center, Southern Florida State University

The trip to the Bahamas was disastrous. Even under 24-hour care and monitoring, the infant beaked whale in captivity at the Atlantis Hotel faded rapidly. Roy Jackson had pressed Simon to stay longer. But for what? To sit around and watch another helpless victim die?

On the plane ride home, Simon Greene had begun filing a suit against the United States Navy for presumable damages incurred from an active sonar test of a submarine purported to be in the vicinity before the strandings. But the suit would have to be put on hold temporarily.

Tonight was his night. He wouldn't miss it for the world.

Kristen Weber poked her head in the office door, asking, "You sure you don't need any help this evening?" Her pale face suggested otherwise; she merely asked as a formality.

Besides, Simon had been looking forward to this moment since his first whale watching trip that summer in the Gulf of Maine when the mother humpback stared directly at him, her eyes filled with intelligence and understanding. He expected tonight–tapping into the eyesight and hearing of his prized bottlenose dolphin, Allie–to rival that experience in a way none other had done so far. It promised to be far too personal to share with anyone, even his graduate student. There would be ample time for his research team to analyze the results later as they spent the next few months pouring over the data.

"No, thanks. I'll be fine," Simon reassured her. "I'll see you in the morning so we can discuss the video footage and audio feed, then run it through the new program."

A wave of relief passed over Kristen's face as she closed the door behind her. Poor girl, Simon thought, stroking his salt-and-pepper goatee, perhaps I've been working her too hard lately. Simon never intended his penchant for perfection in research to negatively impact his grad students. He'd seen all too many burnouts pass through other departments, spending long hours every weekend for their workaholic mentors. Had he unwittingly become a slave driver as well? So obsessed with the upgrade to 7G that he hadn't thought about the needs of his own research assistants?

Well, there'd be plenty of time to change that in the future, Simon decided as he made his final preparations. Only a few minutes remained before the National Conversion. He could analyze his conscience at a later date and make amends where necessary. Perhaps after his research paper was published in the elite Science Journal for his revolutionary breakthroughs in interspecies communication between humans and dolphins.

As Simon glanced up at the video footage of Allie streaming in across the large television monitor centered in his office, a smug smile flickered across his lips. Although he'd minimized the same video in the upper left corner of his eye DOTS, he wanted to display her image on the large screen as well, just in case he lost video feed in the middle of the Conversion due to some unexpected programming glitch.

Allie's undulating body movement appeared normal, even with her modified ear and eye DOTS securely in place. Powered by her muscular caudal peduncle, her tail flukes thrust up and down through the water column. She dove downward, trailing a stream of bubbles in her wake as she sought a dive ring from one of the many toys Simon had scattered in her tank earlier that afternoon. With her mouth turned up in a bottlenose's characteristic grin, she scooped up a canary yellow ring with her rostrum then casually drifted to the surface, a loud exhalation escaping her blowhole. She playfully tossed the ring ahead of her before chasing after it once more.

Simon's eyes flickered to the lime green clock in the upper right corner of his peripheral vision, anxiously watching the seconds tick away. Ten. Nine. Eight. Beads of sweat broke across Simon's brow, despite the lingering chill of his air-conditioned office. Seven. Six. Five. He swallowed hard, his throat tightening with anticipation. Four. Three. Two. Simon closed his eyes. Waiting.

One.

Instantly, Simon heard a train of high-frequency clicks directed at a basketball bobbing on the wavy surface of the tank. Without visual confirmation of the object, he sensed it was spherical in shape by the scattering of sound waves off its rounded surface. The reflected sound waves returned, transmitted through Allie's lower jaw to her inner ear. Much like a hammerhead shark's unusually shaped head, the asymmetrical arrangement of her teeth provided insight to the precise location of the desired object. The high-pitched sounds returned at shorter intervals as she neared the ball, until halting altogether when contact was made. Opening his eyes in awe, Simon now clearly saw the basketball balanced neatly on the tip of Allie's rostrum, but from her perspective.

Chirps of glee resonated through his ear DOTS as she expressed her enthusiasm for her new toy, now grasped firmly between her conical teeth. Simply amazing, Simon beamed as he watched the orange globe sink, then rise, sink, and rise again as Allie performed her own behavior of dribbling the ball around the perimeter of the tank.

The research implications for his new software were remarkable. Now scientists all over the world would have the opportunity to study whales and dolphins in their own watery realm firsthand. The unsolved mysteries of the deep diving sperm whales or migrating humpback populations could be easily revealed with this revolutionary application. The International Whaling Commission could use the evidence to finally create a lasting moratorium on commercial whaling. Why, even tourism could prosper–allowing visitors to experience whale watches and aquariums in a whole new interactive aspect. Not only would this bring Simon fame, he imagined, but great wealth. He settled back into his seat, reveling in the sensation of swimming as if he himself had transformed into this phenomenal streamlined creature.

A sudden loud noise drove Simon straight up in his chair. He clamped his hands over his ears, failing to muffle the excruciating pain within his eardrums. Could this be the echolocation pulse some dolphins used to stun prey? Had he forgotten to account for automatically dampening the wave amplitudes in the event of sudden volume fluctuations? Simon's head reeled and his ears rang, throbbing uncontrollably. Detecting a slow trickle of moistness seeping from his ears, Simon pulled his hands away, gasping in horror.

His palms were covered in blood.

Hearing loss, no doubt, Simon feared. How could he have been so careless? He yanked off the ear DOTS, but it was too late. The sounds from the television monitor had already deadened. Permanently, perhaps.

But before he could curse his own folly, his eyes begin to twinge, shooting daggers of pain into each cornea. No, he thought, this isn't due to echolocation. It was something else.

Simon's eyes began to twitch at a frenzied pace. He'd seen the eye shakes in some of his students before: compulsive gamers whose eyes darted rapidly as they zoomed from one control to another on their optical keyboards. Was this what it felt like?

The pain drove deep into his skull. No...it couldn't be. This was far worse.

Then it hit him. 7G: The new upgrade.

Had the programmers suddenly boosted 7G's frequency to compensate for the global community tapping into our telecommunications technology? Had they the foresight to test this increased power on human subjects before releasing it tonight?

Simon guessed that was a 'no.' And now he would suffer from permanent damage as a result of their imprudence.

Only the pain began to escalate. This isn't the shakes at all, Simon decided as the pressure inside his skull mounted. More like cerebral hemorrhaging. His thoughts immediately flickered back to the stranded pilot and beaked whales, bleeding from their ears and melons. Then to Allie.

He looked up at the computer feed. She had stopped swimming.

Allie.

If he could get his eye DOTS out in time, there was a chance he could still save her. Desperate, Simon pulled back his eyelids, but the spasms prevented him from gripping the DOTS. Drops of blood splattered onto his desk. "Oh, God,"

Simon moaned. He stared at his fingertips...soaked in his own blood.

He glanced back at the video feed streaming uninterrupted through the monitor. Squinting through the agony he endured, Simon glimpsed Allie's inert body slowly sink toward the bottom of the tank, dorsal fin first. Her abandoned basketball automatically rose to the surface, bobbing in her wake. It was too late for her. A fleeting thought passed through his mind: a hope that some type of afterlife existed for his aquatic friend and research subject.

Then Simon slumped forward onto his office desk. Streams of crimson blood oozed from his eyes and ears, seeping between the cracks of his outdated desktop keyboard.

Chapter Twenty

Southern Florida State University off-campus housing

Kristen sulked on the couch, alone. It wasn't like she didn't have anywhere to go, she just preferred solitude at the moment. She'd turned down her roommates' offer to go barhopping that evening. No need to arouse their suspicions by refusing drinks at each stop. And thankfully, Simon Greene gave here the night off. But sitting here, mulling over past decisions wasn't exactly helping her situation.

She'd made a huge mistake telling Dane. All this time she thought picking up where they'd left off would rekindle their relationship. Not destroy it altogether.

The narcissistic, egomaniacal coward, she thought with disgust. He'd spent that entire weekend talking about himself. Never asked a single question about her research, had he? He had no intention of settling down and starting a family–not when he was too wrapped up in his own power trip to think of anyone but himself. Get real, Dane–it's just an internship for God's sake.

Then, after she'd told him, he had the audacity to reply with the accusation, "Are you sure it's mine?" And that was the last she'd heard from him.

How cruel and insensitive could you be? Well, better she find that out now than after a trip down the aisle. Besides, she wasn't due until spring. She could finish out the semester, then take some time off. Get a second job to pay for day care if she must. Somehow, she'd find a way to make it work. After all, she wasn't the first woman in history to struggle as a single mom.

Besides, she knew she could count on Erik for support. Once she got around to telling him, that is. But not yet. Not until she started to show. That would give her some time to make a plan.

Speaking of which, why wasn't Erik replying to any of her texts, either? What was it with her and guys?

Sick of pathetically waiting for someone to send her an optical message, she turned on the old plasma T.V. She couldn't bear to stream a video on her eye DOTS and not receive any messages from Dane. Sure, he'd be busy tonight with the online debut of Dreamscape, but something inside her sensed she would've received the same response, regardless of when she announced the news. What a weak, spineless excuse for a boyfriend. So they were completely over now. She'd have to do this on her own.

"What's your MUDE?" the television piped to a hip-hop tune, advertising bling mobile uplinks. This certainly wasn't helping her forget Dane.

Kristen snatched the remote off the coffee table and began flipping through the channels, eventually settling on a movie station that offered no commercial interruptions. Still, it did little to distract her. She struggled to follow the plot, but it was no use. Her thoughts kept returning to her uncertain future and the disappointing revelation of Dane's true self.

Soon her ears started ringing and her head began to spin. This stress couldn't be good for the pregnancy. Especially when she was too upset to eat dinner tonight.

Kristen pulled her tired body off the couch and rose to her feet. Only the headache instantly worsened. Her eyes began to pulsate, like an irrepressible nervous twitch times ten. She bent over, steadying herself on the arm of the couch and placing her free hand against her pounding temple. Rich, red drops splattered the surface of the coffee table. Kristen stared at them incomprehensibly; unable to register they belonged to her.

The world grew red as it spun madly; the room seemed to revolve upside down. Blinded, Kristen fell to the floor, whacking her head against the corner of the coffee table. She strained to reach the wound, wet and sticky to the touch. When she pulled her fingers away, Kristen realized why.

Her hand was soaked with blood.

Not only had her headache intensified to unimaginable proportions, but the mounting pressure inside her eyes and ears made her skull feel like it was about to explode. A powerful urge to protect her unborn fetus suddenly overcame Kristen. As her body entered a wave of uncontrolled spasms, she expended her remaining energy toward touching her abdomen, cradling the unborn child she'd never have the opportunity to call her own.

Then her hand fell limp to the floor, leaving five long streaks of blood across her white shirt.

Chapter Twenty-One

Quarantine Room, U.S.S. Siren

"Arrghhh!" Alyssa Kensington grunted, rolling over on the mattress and stuffing the pillow over her head. "I can't take it any more!" How many times had she relived that moment, wishing the interruption had never occurred? Otherwise, how might their evening have ended? Would she have had the willpower to stop?

Hours later, she'd bumped into Justin Hidalgo in the hall–accompanied by three other officers. All were completely soaked, dripping water down the grated floor with each step. Alyssa barely recognized Justin at first. Wet and exhausted, his eyes lackluster, he acknowledged her with a meager, tired nod as he passed.

Not daring to speak lest the others detect the rising blush in her cheeks, she stood at attention against the wall, secretly trying to read Justin's expression. She didn't dare text him to apologize for their botched evening. There could be no electronic documentation of their encounter.

Since then, she hadn't had the chance to see him privately. In the halls, Justin rushed past her. And in the crowded Mess Hall, he sat with the other officers from their shift. Even when she saw him at her station in the Command and Control Room, his manners were curt. Was he merely afraid to arouse suspicion? Was he intentionally avoiding her? Or did he regret his actions, wishing he could change the past?

Plagued with indecision, Alyssa sat up and stretched. She knew she wouldn't be able to rest again with her mind in overdrive. Besides, how long had she been stuck in quarantine already? Without the clock from her eye DOTS, she could only guess that another three hours had passed by. Probably time for more drops. Reaching over to grab the bottle of sulfacetamide from the sink, she suddenly realized something. Without a clock, how would she know her three days had elapsed? Would someone come to relieve her? Or would they expect her to return to work on her own? Alyssa chided herself for not thinking to ask Medical Officer Knolls that question beforehand.

Lying down again, she stared at the ceiling, willing herself to think about anything but Justin. Her stiff body ached from lack of movement. Earlier, she stowed the mattress away, completing more sets of push-ups and stomach crunches on the floor than her muscles desired, but it wasn't enough. She really needed to stand and walk around–outside of this boring room. Unfortunately, that was impossible until her release.

Hour after monotonous hour passed. How long had it been? One full day? Two? It was impossible to say. She tried to recall the number of times she'd slept and how many meals she'd been served–yet between breakfast, lunch, dinner, and midnight rations, everything blended together. The overwhelming claustrophobia of this confining metallic space had already seeped in, making her dizzy and nauseous.

Repeatedly, she questioned Justin's actions toward her. And she cursed her hormones for getting the best of her resolve.

Alyssa realized she had to get out of Quarantine before she lost it–despite Medical Officer Knolls' assignment here for three days. She knew she ought to obey a direct command, but at what expense?

Twiddling her thumbs, Alyssa pondered the ramifications of breaking her confinement. The Commander and XO wouldn't want her inept for the remainder of the tour of duty, right? Surely, she must do something to prevent herself from going mentally insane. But where could Alyssa go without exposing others to the contagious pathogen she harbored?

There was only one place: the gym.

Just don't let me bump into Justin again, Alyssa fretted. Now that he knows I've been quarantined, how would he react? Would he have the cohones to report me to the XO?

Hell, yes.

Indecisive, Alyssa deliberated to the point of making herself sick. One fact was certain–she couldn't stay here any longer. She'd have to deal with the repercussions for disobeying an order, however awful they might be. After placing the drops in her eyes once more, she stowed the bottle inside the chest pocket of her navy blue work uniform and buttoned it shut. With renewed determination, Alyssa cracked the door to check for any passersby, then slipped out. And prayed she wouldn't run into Officers Knolls or Hidalgo.

Keeping her head down in the tight hallways, Alyssa squished her back against the wall to let the other submariners pass. She mumbled a greeting while intentionally covering her last name with her arm. Alyssa hoped the gesture seemed inconspicuous. She hoped they didn't notice her reddened eyes.

Afraid of returning to her berth to grab gym clothes, Alyssa decided to exercise in the same work uniform she wore when assigned to Quarantine. Besides, she already had her running shoes. Ever mindful of the Siren's sound signature in the water, submariners always wore soft-soled running shoes or sneakers.

Not that it really mattered. She shouldn't be here anyway.

Squeezing through the knee-knocking watertight door to enter the gymnasium, she crinkled her nose in the cold, metallic air rank with stale sweat. Crammed with a nautilus set, punching bag, and a few treadmills, even this small gymnasium sat fully enclosed in sound-dampening protection.

However, much to Alyssa's surprise, the room stood empty. The rest of the crew must be momentarily preoccupied with working, eating, or sleeping. She hoped it would remain that way.

Turning on the treadmill, Alyssa stretched out her legs at a slow, steady gait. Her cramped legs and arms resisted at first, but after the first mile, she managed to work out most of the kinks in her joints. Though she would have preferred some music to fill the empty void, she didn't have her DOTS. Instead, she sufficed with the rhythmic trod of her feet against the revolving belt blending with her pattern of regular breaths.

Her muscles feeling loose once more, Alyssa pumped her arms back and forth and increased her pace. Finally, she could breathe again, relieved to be outside the miniscule Quarantine Room. Eventually desensitized to the smell of the gym, she closed her eyes, envisioning the familiar scenery from her old running routes back home...

Lush hills covered in farmland rolled along the horizon. Wispy clouds sailed across a pale blue sky. Overhead, half a dozen turkey vultures soared, their feeble V-shaped wings tipping suddenly when they caught a rising updraft. From their lofty heights, the vultures scanned the ground below for road kill along Highway 29 snaking south to Charlottesville. The bleak interior of the submarine's gymnasium soon dissolved into the familiar silhouettes of the Blue Ridge Mountains in Shenandoah National Park, the backdrop to her cozy little town of Madison, Virginia.

Alyssa dredged up memories of running down forested trails with rich scents of pine and spruce hanging in the air as their treetops obscured the sky. Or the sugary aroma of the honeysuckle bush in their yard as she sprinted for home. Instead of dashing inside for a glass of water, she'd let the sweat pour off her while savoring the long stamens' drips of nectar concealed within each blossom. She even missed the nose-crinkling odor of her golden retriever, Tucker, muddy from playing in the creek, as he charged across the lawn to greet her. She'd brush his matted tail and belly free of hitchhiker seed pods, then bathe him before permitting him inside the house.

Opening her eyes, Alyssa visualized the treadmill as a track winding through a field of Black-eyed Susan and Queen Anne's lace wildflowers that swayed in the warm, humid breeze. Young green sumac and tall tan grasses flowed freely, only beginning to lose their chlorophyll in their annual transformation into the robust shades of cranberry red and bright gold that adorned the countryside, a precursor to the autumnal foliage's explosion of color.

She closed her eyes again, this time imagining the rosy hues of the setting sun filling the valley, casting an orange glow over the rustic farmhouses and silos. The austere, cold interior of the submarine was a stark contrast to her previous existence. Recently, her memories of home had intensified as she desperately fought her recurring bouts of depression. The gym was her favorite area of escape. The only area aboard the Siren where she could pretend she was somewhere else.

And the only way to survive the upcoming long months of her tour of duty.

Alyssa continued to replay scenes from home: hiking with Tucker through the wooded trails of Shenandoah or sitting on the back deck to watch the sun set below the mountaintops. She pushed herself to run full-speed now, beads of sweat breaking out across her brow and trickling down the sides of her cheeks. Perspiration erupted across her back and stained the armpits of her uniform.

Endorphins coursed through Alyssa's veins, alleviating her guilt of presumably causing the unnecessary and premature deaths of those unfortunate marine mammals with the push of a button. She ceased blaming herself for the possible epidemic of conjunctivitis she initiated. She no longer felt the need to overanalyze Justin's actions. If he wanted to see her again, let him find a way to make it happen.

Careful to avoid touching her contagious eyes, Alyssa wiped away the sweat and released a heavy sigh. Finally, she felt freed. Released from the anchor of culpability tied to her ankles, threatening to drag her into the abyss of despair.

Then the path sloped, gradually at first. Alyssa's shins hammered as she lengthened her stride to compensate for the uneven terrain. Pumping her arms softer now, she tried to slow her momentum as she ran downhill.

Hang on, Alyssa thought as she stopped running altogether. Panting, she gripped the handrails, trying to make sense of her surroundings.

Downhill?

What was going on?

The floor tilted backwards beneath her feet, making her lean slightly. Why would they be conducting maneuvers now? And at this depth?

Was it possible they'd been attacked?

She recalled the Siren's initial descent to periscope depth, seventy-five feet below the surface. There the floor had inclined at a 35-degree angle while the crew double-checked for flooding before daring to descend further. Only at the time, she was prepared, bracing herself against the wall as the sub rolled fore and aft.

But now, she had no advance knowledge. How could she when–without her DOTS–she'd been cut off from communication with the rest of the crew?

"Better get outta here," Alyssa muttered to herself as she turned off the treadmill. Arms extended for balance, she stumbled across the slanted floor, grasping the nautilus bars for support, then ducked through the watertight hatch to head back to Quarantine…hopefully before someone noticed her missing.

Stricken with fear, she hurried through the corridors, frightened of getting caught out of her Quarantine room. Would they honestly believe her excuse for leaving? That she was simply preventing herself from going insane? That she only tried to escape the dismal void of unchecked depression that consumed the life of one seaman already this voyage?

Justin might. But she couldn't count on the others.

And she had reason to worry. She'd seen the effect of the XO's corporal punishments on Siren crewmates who crossed the line.

Alyssa peered into the darkness around the next corner, briefly hesitating before entering the hallway. Fortunately, no one seemed to be working on any repairs in this area at the moment. She hustled down the narrow passageway, praying she could make it back to her assigned room without encountering anyone.

Although she lacked the clear night vision of her eye DOTS, she felt more accustomed to using her natural eyesight again. How long had it been since she'd relied solely on her naked eyes? She marveled at their inefficiency, after months of functioning under the military's version of optimal vision.

The sub lurched forward, causing Alyssa to lose her balance. She slammed into the wall, bruising her shoulder. Cautiously, Alyssa got back to her feet, gripping objects along the wall to support herself from sliding downward. She passed the next open doorway leading to the Command and Control Room and paused.

Instead of the typical periwinkle blue background lighting bathing the controls, the room flashed red in alarm. Alyssa gasped, clamping her hand over her mouth as she surveyed her crewmates.

Something had gone terribly wrong.

The room was littered with bodies.

Chapter Twenty-Two

"What the hell—?" Alyssa stared in disbelief at the officers collapsed upon the ground, the helmsman and crew slumped over their computer screens and gauges. The coppery smell of fresh blood lingered in the air.

Confused, she raced across the slanted floor to the helmsman, his body pressed forward against the controls. Shoving him out of the way, she yanked back on the controls with all her might in a desperate attempt to right the submarine's unplanned descent. Nothing happened; the sub stayed its dangerous course downward.

Alyssa assumed the alarm had activated a security measure, locking her out of the system. Without an officer's code card, she could not alter the Siren's new course.

She kneeled to search the pockets of the officer lying face down on the floor near the helmsman. She tried the fallen XO, too, but couldn't locate his code card. Thinking quickly, she leaped over another body to access her sonar station and send out a Morse Code message requesting help. Perspiration dripped from her brow as she found the archaic device-intended only as a backup measure-and began tapping the identifiable sequence of three short dots, three long dashes, then three short dots again.

S–O–S. The international distress call.

Someone must be nearby to receive her call for help. Fingers flying across the keys, she programmed the computer to repeat the message indefinitely. It was only a matter of time before they'd be discovered.

Rather than wait for a response, Alyssa bolted from the Command and Control Room, sliding down the steep grade of the hall as she screamed to alert the others. Now she understood why the sub had shifted from its normal course. But she couldn't get it back on track by herself.

Upon reaching the crews' quarters in the berthing area, she dashed inside the first room where nine enlisted men lay berthed in rows of three along each wall. One man's arm dangled outside his curtain.

Bracing herself on the slanted floor, she threw open the privacy curtain and forcefully shook the slumbering submariner, trying to rouse him. "Wake up! Please!" she implored. "I need your help!" His body felt like a lead weight, impossible to move.

Keeping one hand on the railing to steady herself, she bent down toward the man on the lowest rack, shouting again. Slowly, the man's head rolled toward her, but he didn't wake. Alyssa leaned closer, ready to shake him once more. Then, in the dim light, she noticed something unusual about him. What was that smeared across his face?

A black liquid trickled from his eyes and ears, staining his white pillowcase.

Alyssa stared at him in confusion for several seconds before goose bumps exploded down the length of her arms and up the back of her spine.

She realized the identity of the black liquid.

At depths greater than 30 feet underwater, short wavelengths of visible light in the red spectrum are readily absorbed, giving red objects a dark gray or black appearance. After their initial descent, she remembered noticing that the red toothbrush from her bag of toiletries no longer looked the same. Deep below the surface, it appeared nearly black.

Alyssa also remembered vacationing with her mother at Universal Studios in Orlando, Florida many years ago. Her mom had needed a break from the sizzling midday sun, zooming roller coasters, and whirling amusement park rides, so she dragged Alyssa inside the Alfred Hitchcock Theater. At the time, Alyssa'd never heard of the filmmaker, famous for his suspenseful, psychological thrillers.

Although she had little interest in the old-fashioned screenplays, there was one fact that remained in her long-term memory all these years. The presenter explained how many types of objects appeared different in the old black and white films than in later color sequences. So when Alfred Hitchcock directed the original Psycho movie, he experimented with a variety of liquids in the graphic shower scene. Eventually he selected chocolate sauce to make the violent attack seem more realistic.

On the movie clip, the chocolate sauce looked identical to the liquid that now seeped from the seaman's eyeballs and ear canals.

But Alyssa knew this was no special effect aimed at terrifying a movie audience.

This was real.

The man's face was covered in blood.

Chapter Twenty-Three

"Oh, dear God!" Alyssa shouted, unconcerned with awakening the other tired submariners or the consequences of her leaving her assigned quarantine area. This man needed immediate medical attention. "Someone...HELP ME! PLEASE!"

Naturally, she expected an instant reaction. After all, eight other submariners currently slept in this small area. Why wasn't anyone coming to her aid?

She turned toward the man again. She didn't recognize him from the Mess Hall or her station, so he must've been assigned to another shift. What could've happened to him? Had he hit his head on the rack above when the sub tilted downward, causing a brain hemorrhage? She placed her index and middle finger together along his jugular, feeling for a pulse.

Then Alyssa recoiled in horror. The skin beneath her fingertips was lifeless. She was too late; he was already terminal.

Stepping back, she steadied herself against the rack, unfamiliar with the sensation of witnessing death firsthand. It was easier to cope with at her grandmother's funeral. The woman had lived a long, satisfying life. Seeing her body in the open casket–with heaps of makeup applied to her embalmed body — made her look far different than the actual Gran. More like a wax impression of the vibrant person she'd known from her childhood.

But this was real. And there was nothing she could do to help this young, unfortunate submariner.

Stunned, Alyssa shook the sleeping body on the lowest rack, trying to wake up this man as well. But when she rolled him over, Alyssa found the same blank, bloody stare. In fact, everyone here was bleeding from the eyes and ears.

All of them were dead.

In shock, she backed out of the room, hoping to find help elsewhere. Yet the adjacent rooms wielded the same results. Ducking her head under the exposed pipes, she scanned the racks for survivors.

She found none.

What had happened to the crew while she was in the gym? What kind of destructive force caused such widespread devastation throughout the sub? Unable to locate any other signs of life, Alyssa staggered up the steep grade of the hallway, hand over hand on the railing. Eventually, she stumbled back to her station in the Command and Control Room, oblivious to the bumps and bruises she'd incurred as a result of her unaided vision and the skewed floor of the sinking ship.

Above the cacophony of the room's wailing alarm and pulsating red lights, her station seemed eerily calm. Filling the blank computer screen, the Morse Code sequence of dot-dot-dot, dash-dash-dash, dot-dot-dot continued to repeat itself.

Alyssa stared at the blinking cursor.

• • • − − − • • •

• • • − − − • • •

• • • − − − • • •

7G

Grabbing the mouse, she scrolled backwards, searching...
In vain.

She'd received no response from the outside world.

"Impossible," Alyssa breathed, realizing her hopes of a Deep Submergence Rescue Vehicle coming to her aid were dashed. "No one is coming."

No one. The words echoed in her skull.

She'd never felt so alone in her entire life.

Panic gripped Alyssa's throat, choking her every breath. Her heart rate escalated, as if her ribs could not contain its surging power. Alyssa stood frozen with fear, like a White-tailed deer caught in a speeding car's headlights on a dark, wooded road. So this was it? Her final hurrah? She gasped, but the stale cabin air provided ill reprieve.

Gripping the back of her chair, Alyssa struggled to regain control of her emotions. They were still headed downward. And if she didn't do something soon, she too would remain trapped inside this submarine of death until it crashed upon the seabed, with no hope of rescue.

"NO!" Alyssa shrieked, digging her nails into her palms to jar herself back to reality. This is NOT my fate.

Clarity restored, Alyssa knew somehow she must escape, reach the surface, and notify naval authorities to salvage the sub. Otherwise, all her colleagues would be lost forever, lacking proper military burials. Alyssa imagined their families back home, mourning the loss of their loved ones. She envisioned their funeral processions bearing empty coffins draped in the Stars and Stripes. The ceremonial flag folding that followed, a humble parting gift to the seaman's mother in exchange for the life of her child.

They deserved so much more.

Then Alyssa remembered her own mother. The promise she'd made on Send-Off Day that everything would be okay.

That she would return home.

Her face turned grave as she contemplated her fate. This wasn't just about a broken promise. This was about her future. And she knew her future could not exist here, trapped beneath the ocean.

Forever.

"I've gotta get out of here. NOW." Renewed determination flooded Alyssa's veins as she suddenly recalled one particular aspect from her submarine training at Groton's Sub School.

An enormous tower filled with water, simulating the egress escape chamber.

"Of course! There's still a last resort!" she exclaimed. Alyssa spun around to check the depth gauge. Her grin faded as she watched the numbers increase.

Three eighty. Three ninety. Four hundred feet...and dropping.

Not good. Gingerly, Alyssa stepped over the bodies of her crewmates on the floor. Immediately, bile rose up her throat. Clamping one hand over her mouth, she clutched her stomach as she recognized Carly Zapelli turned upwards, staring at the ceiling. Carly's cropped black hair spilled out from under her U.S.S. Siren cap. Sticky black blood oozed from her eye sockets. Carly had completed basic training with her. And now...

Focus, Alyssa. There will be plenty of time for remembering Carly later. You'll do her no good if you can't get out yourself.

Grasping the periscope shafts for support, Alyssa tiptoed over Carly's torso toward the light table documenting the Siren's course. She leaned over the illuminated paper, examining the bathymetric chart of the Florida coast. Despite recent technological advances, the Navy still relied on this paper and marker technique to plot their course since it was readily accessible in the event of computer glitches. Using her index finger, Alyssa tracked their route, a series of Xs connected by hatched lines depicting the Siren's passage across the Caribbean and into the Atlantic Ocean.

"My God, it's steep," Alyssa muttered, noticing the close proximity of the contour lines. Off the west coast of Florida, the shallow waters of the continental shelf spread far into the Caribbean Sea. But here at their current location off southeast Florida, the shelf hugged the coastline...while the sea floor plummeted down the continental slope toward the abyssal plain. She wouldn't have to worry about a shock wave rippling through the hull of sub when it collided with the benthic sediment on the sea floor. Not when the floor dropped thousands of feet.

Thousands, Alyssa thought grimly.

In training, they'd told her that escape was limited to depths above 600 feet. Alyssa hunched over the light table, tracing her finger along their current trajectory, wondering how deep they could dive. "Five hundred, five-twenty–" she murmured to herself. But before she reached five hundred forty feet in depth, her finger ran across a black splotch that pooled over the area. Dark like India ink. Smearing it across the paper affixed to the light table, she realized it wasn't marker. Marker wasn't sticky.

As Alyssa rubbed the substance off on the back of her pant leg, she accidentally bumped into a figure collapsed upon the table. His head lolled to one side, smearing blood across his features. Alyssa swore under her breath as she stared in shock at the submariner. His insignia signified an officer. But with his eyes glazed in the blackened substance, they were unrecognizable.

119

Yet something about his bloodstained face seemed uncannily familiar. Before Alyssa could make the connection, she noticed the name embroidered upon the patch across his chest.

HIDALGO.

"No. No," Alyssa moaned, backing away in horror. "It can't be!"

Not Justin. It wasn't fair! He had such a promising future, a future she had hoped to share with him. And she never even had a chance to say goodbye. Their brief conversation in the hallway on her way to Quarantine was the last time she ever saw him…alive. A single tear rolled down her cheek.

Making a vow to locate his family, she slipped off the dolphin fish pin centered above his left breast pocket, studying the distinguished submariner badge in her hand. The gold-plated bronze pin depicted two dolphin fish–with rectangular heads, bulbous eyes, and tails curled over their backs–rising out of the water, flanking the starboard and port sides of a submarine's bow and conning tower. She glanced down at her own uniform with the same design embroidered in silk.

Justin was respectable. He deserved recognition for the ultimate sacrifice he gave his country…buried beneath a white marble headstone at Arlington National Cemetery.

They all deserved that much.

And that would never happen unless she managed to escape.

With one last glance at Justin, Alyssa realized the time had come. She stowed his pin in her pocket for safekeeping and squared her shoulders, renewing her resolve to get out of here.

Now.

Or like the other 138 seamen aboard, the Siren would become her sunken tomb as well.

Chapter Twenty-Four

Horace T. Ross Library, Southern Florida State University

Erik Weber woke to sunlight streaming through the blinds of the library windows. How long had he been here? And why didn't they wake him when the library closed? They did close for the night, didn't they? Erik couldn't say for sure; he'd never pulled an all-nighter before. Not for studying, at least.

Wiping the spittle from the corner of his mouth, he stretched to work the kinks out of his neck and back, then ran his fingers through his disheveled sandy blonde hair. At least he felt better rested for confronting Rachael. No, not confronting, he reminded himself. That would immediately put her on the defensive. He'd better find a new angle or he'd never mend their relationship. He loved her, right? So why not start off with an apology? For what he did wrong. The problem was he still didn't know what he'd done to drive her away in the first place. Okay, so leave it vague and play it by ear. Whatever it takes, he reminded himself. Whatever it takes.

Satisfied with his plan, he pushed the chair backwards to leave. Glancing around the library, he noticed that the other

Friday night library geeks had fallen asleep at their desks, too. "So much for turbo-studying," he chuckled under his breath as he exited the room.

Erik was mildly surprised to find the library clerk's desk empty as he passed. Didn't they always have someone manning this station? Then again, with budget cuts across campus, they couldn't afford to hire two people for the same shift. Even the clerk's gotta take a whiz sometimes.

Pushing open the heavy double doors to leave, Erik peeked over his shoulder. His skin prickled as he spotted a shoe sticking out from behind the clerk's desk. Erik let the door swing closed and wandered back for a better look.

The same library clerk from last night lay unconscious behind the clerk's desk. "You okay?" Erik asked, kneeling beside his inert body. His pockmarked face lay covered with thick, black hair. Erik nudged the kid's shoulders, trying to rouse him. Nothing. Then he shook him more forcefully. A few strands of the kid's hair slid off his face, revealing glassy eyes smothered in flaky, dried blood.

Erik realized why the clerk was unresponsive.

He was dead.

Mute from shock, Erik backed away. He should probably tell someone like Campus Security or something. But his fingerprints were all over the kid. Would they detain Erik as a suspect, thinking that he had killed this kid?

Heart racing, Erik fled the library steps. He had a good alibi. He'd fallen asleep and found the kid this morning. The blood was old so it must've happened hours ago.

Then he remembered something. He hadn't told anyone he was coming here. In fact, he wasn't sure the other two people in the library could vouch for him ever being there. And his only witness lay dead on the floor.

Erik finally understood how people could be wrongly accused of a crime.

Enveloped in tunnel vision, Erik raced across the Arts Quad, trying to piece together the sequence of events. He'd only gone there to escape Rachael's incessant texting and take a short nap. And now look what happened! This wasn't how he'd planned to win Rachael back. She'd probably hate him even more after he told her. But at the moment, he needed her logic and reason. She'd know what he should do. She'd believe he was innocent, wouldn't she?

"Of course she will," Erik convinced himself as he sped down the hill to their dorm.

With his brain in overdrive, Erik didn't notice the eerie stillness that hung over the university campus, even for a Saturday morning. He saw a few undergrads lying on the grass near the dorm entrance. Probably passed out, Erik figured as his nervous fingers fumbled with the key to their dorm. It wasn't the first time.

Flying down the hall, Erik stopped in front of Rachael's single room and rapped his knuckles on the door, waiting for an answer. He knocked louder this time, not caring if he woke up anyone else. This was urgent.

"Where is she?" Erik muttered as he knocked a third time. "You don't think–?"

Visions of Rachael with that tall, muscular, D-1 football player filled his head. But she had a single room. Wouldn't she just bring him back here? Unless she was afraid of bumping into Erik.

Erik's heart filled with a new sense of dread. His head tipped forward, hitting her wooden door. Time to face the fact that she'd spent the night in another guy's room. Not only had he officially lost her, he had to face the consequences of the dead clerk alone.

Erik's feet wobbled beneath him. He gripped her doorknob to steady himself. Strangely, the doorknob turned.

She's here! Erik thought as renewed hope filled his soul. As a running joke, Erik liked to tease her about ritually locking her room. Rachael never left her door open, claiming it was instinct for her to lock up whenever she left. She was from New York.

"Rachael?" he asked, slowly opening the door. Sure enough, she was sprawled across the bed, still dressed in her clothes from last night. Erik felt a slight pang of guilt for not being there to ensure she got home safely. It reminded him of the first time he walked her home from the Sigma Delt party.

Then Erik spotted him: the football player. He lay crashed out, his large frame squeezed into her little chair. Though he slept facing the wall, Erik recognized him immediately. So she'd brought the guy back here last night after all.

Before he woke either of them, Erik turned to leave and tripped over a pillow lying near her desk.

A pillow? Erik didn't want to know how that'd gotten on the floor. Filled with dismay, he stepped back into the hall, taking one last glimpse of the scene, though he knew he'd never forget it.

His head drooped as he closed the door behind him. Then he noticed something else lying on the floor by the pillow...a sleeping bag.

A sleeping bag? Why would Rachael pull out a sleeping bag for her new boyfriend?

Erik creaked open the door again, his eyes trained on the guy. Long rays of morning sunlight touched a golden charm dangling from the kid's neck. "At least he's a sound sleeper," Erik muttered as he tiptoed closer to look at the charm. It was one of those customized new MUDEs for 7G. The kind of

Debbie Kump

mobile uplink you'd wear around your neck to keep your pockets free.

Erik bent closer, squinting at the writing that read J ME. Sure, lots of people personalized their new MUDEs with logos of their favorite sports teams, brand names, clip art, even engraved photos. But J ME? That's more like something off a designer license plate, Erik thought as he repeated the phrase again and again in his head.

Then it hit him.

"Oh, no," Erik moaned. How dense could he be? Rachael'd said her prefrosh cousin, Jamie, was coming up for the weekend. All this time he'd simply assumed Jamie was a girl. Not some tall, athletic guy that looked nothing like her.

"I'm so sorry, Rachael," he apologized, hugging her in her sleep as he whispered in her ear. "I had no idea." He pulled her close, grateful to have her back. There'd never been another guy. No cheating, either. How could he have been such an idiot to not listen to her, to grow so jealous over nothing? Well, there'd be plenty of time to mend the past. Heck, maybe she'd enjoy a good laugh over his naiveté.

Infused with relief, Erik tightened his embrace, only Rachael didn't move. Now that he thought about it, Erik hadn't seen her chest rise and fall as she slumbered, had he?

Suddenly, Erik's face darkened. "Rachael?" he breathed as he rolled her slumbering body to face him.

Her head drooped to one side, settling against her shoulder. Her typically vivacious blue eyes were filmed over and caked with blood, lifelessly staring at nothing in particular.

Chapter Twenty-Five

Not Rachael, too!

In an instant, Erik felt his world viciously stripped from him. And to think she died believing he was mad at her. That he didn't love her anymore. Erik crumpled to his knees, burying his face in his hands.

For long minutes, Erik sobbed uncontrollably, unable to think. He'd already forgotten about the dead clerk lying on the floor of the Ross Library, covered in his fingerprints. So was Rachael, for that matter. Yet Erik no longer cared if they charged him for the murders. Nothing seemed important anymore.

But somewhere in the back of his mind, Erik realized that her cousin, Jamie, didn't know. He still slept soundly on the couch. "How can he sleep at a time like this?!" Erik exclaimed.

Gathering himself to his feet, fury built inside of Erik. What had they done last night? And why hadn't Jamie stopped Rachael before she got hurt? Worse than hurt, Erik.

Dead.

Erik's body shook with mounting rage. Yet not all of it was directed at Jamie. Guilt weighed heavily upon Erik's conscience. If only he'd apologized yesterday, then he would've prevented this from happening. He could've been there when she went out to keep an eye on her. She would still be alive.

Torn between pummeling Jamie and cursing his own soul for the remainder of his miserable existence, Erik crossed the small dorm room in three swift steps. Gritting his teeth, he clenched his fists, letting his nails dig deep into his skin. "Still, I've gotta tell him," Erik fumed as he reached out, planning to shake Jamie senseless. Grabbing the kid's shoulder, Erik yanked hard, spinning Jamie to face him.

"Oh. My. God." Erik swore loudly as he staggered backwards, unable to find his feet. How could this be?

The kid's eyes were blackened with blood. Just like Rachael's.

Erik's initial shock was soon replaced with an urgent need to respond. His body tensed suddenly as logic flooded his brain. Regardless of what had happened to them last night, he must call 911 immediately. Only when his eyes darted to the side to activate the virtual keyboard, it was gone. Habitually, he tapped the back pocket of his jeans, but the mobile uplink was missing, too.

All of a sudden, Erik recalled last night's events in startling clarity. Of course—he had left his MUDE and DOTS back on his desk. Flying down the hall to his room, he slammed open the door.

Only to find his roommate, Lucas Smith, face down on the floor...in a puddle of his own blood.

Erik screamed in shock. His hands trembled as he clutched the corner of the desk for support. It wasn't like he and Lucas were best of friends. But still, he wouldn't wish this on anyone. Call for help. Call for help, he reminded himself, though his body felt incapable of moving.

He remembered the school shootings he'd heard about in the past. Waves of violence had swept the country as copycatting disgruntled teens pulled the trigger on their bullying classmates and then on themselves in a final act of revenge. But this was worse. This was indiscriminant. There were no bullet wounds. No gunman slinking around the dorm, either. Besides, that didn't explain the library clerk, dead halfway across campus.

So what could've caused this? Erik shook his head, trying to focus. Though right now, the cause was unimportant. It only mattered that he got help. Spotting his old MUDE and DOTS lying on his desk, he realized he still hadn't called 911.

Lucid once more, Erik reached for an eye DOT, plucking it from the case. But as he lifted the circular disc to place on his pupil, he felt the DOT pulsate on his fingertip.

"Quit shaking", he scolded himself as he steadied his trembling hand for a second attempt.

While lifting the lens to his eyeball, it vibrated off his finger and onto the floor. Erik dropped to his knees, swearing under his breath as he searched for the lens on the carpet in vain. "I don't have time for this," Erik grumbled as he rose to his feet to try the second DOT lens. But it too began to pulsate oddly upon his fingertip. He gripped it tightly, raising it toward his eye. Yet, something didn't seem right. Erik paused for a second with the DOT poised millimeters from his face. A wave of dizziness passed over him. As pressure mounted inside his eyeball, his head screamed in agony.

Erik pulled the lens away, studying it in his hand. Yet even when he held as still as possible considering the traumatic circumstances he'd witnessed, the lens appeared blurry. As if resonating at a high frequency, like a tuning fork touching the surface of a glass of water.

Forget the eye DOTS, Erik thought, setting the lens back in the case. Maybe he could call 911 with his ear DOTS alone. But when he placed one of the circular sticker electronics near his right ear, a deafening ringing sound filled his head. Erik swooned, dropping the ear DOT as he doubled over. He clamped one palm over his ear to alleviate the pain, but it was of no use. The ringing persisted. Then Erik felt a trickle of liquid seep down his cheek. What is that? he wondered, wiping it clean.

"Ahhh!" Erik shrieked as he stared at the blood smeared across his palm. Blood and ringing...this could not be good. Sure, Erik's ears had rung after some of the rock concerts he'd seen on campus, but nothing like this. Holding his hand by his right ear, he snapped his fingers together, but could barely hear the noise. Infuriated, he snapped again and again. Still, the snap was hardly audible, like cotton balls plugged his entire ear canal.

As Erik lashed out to sweep his MUDE and DOTS off the desk, his hand froze in midair. He thought of Jamie's bling MUDE dangling out of his shirt. Then he blinked, a connection suddenly registering in his mind.

Last night was The Conversion. The National Upgrade to 7G Network.

He slammed his fist against the desk. It couldn't be, could it? Don't be ludicrous, Erik. He paused. Was it even possible?

That the new upgrade to 7G actually caused this wave of death?

Consumed with a sudden urge to flee the dorm, he stumbled outside. An unnerving quiet filled the air–and not just from Erik's impaired hearing. Rounding the corner of his dorm, he found more bodies collapsed upon the sidewalks and the path to the dining hall. Familiar faces of people he knew from classes and parties, intramurals and meals. All their faces blemished with the same telltale stains of blood. Everywhere he turned, everyone was dead.

Except for Erik.

And if everyone on campus was dead, that meant...

A new wave of fear gripped Erik. He raced down the street, toward Kristen's apartment.

Chapter Twenty-Six

Erik Weber threw open the door to his sister's apartment, shouting her name. He barreled through the entryway. Inside his head, his screams sounded lopsided, muted on the right. And the apartment oddly silent.

Where could she be? Erik remembered she'd been feeling sick. Surely she'd be here...unless she went to Dr. Greene's office. He'd planned to unveil his new breakthrough last night, hadn't he?

Biting his lip, Erik tentatively opened each bedroom door, finding all the rooms vacant. "Figures," he muttered, "the place is too quiet." She probably wasn't home.

But as he passed the family room, Erik noticed the old plasma screen lit up. A bright blue rectangle displayed the message NO SIGNAL AVAILABLE. He walked toward the T.V. to shut it off when his stomach somersaulted.

He found her.

With blond curls spilling across her face, Kristen's head drooped to one side. Erik fell to his knees, brushing the hair away to gaze into his sister's unresponsive, bloody eyes. How much more of this could he take? He barely had the chance to grieve for Rachael...and now Kristen, too? Tears splashed down his cheeks, falling onto his sister's corpse.

Through his blurry vision, Erik noticed something peculiar about Kristen's position. He blinked, clearing his eyes to gaze upon her form once more.

A red handprint across her abdomen trailed off in long streaks where her fingers dropped to the floor. Almost protective in her attempt to cradle...

To cradle?

Reality hit Erik square in the face. Why didn't he see it before? The plans for a semester off from her beloved graduate program. The distancing from Dane. The repeated bouts of illness. Not the flu at all, was it? More like...

Morning sickness.

Erik was an idiot. He hadn't been there when she'd needed him the most. Too wrapped up in his web of fabricated lies. Obsessed with a cheating girlfriend that never even existed.

Erik planted a gentle kiss upon his sister's forehead, then exited the apartment. He would come back for her later. For all of them. But right now he must find his parents to inform them about Kristen and her unborn child.

Scratch that. His parents were a little old-fashioned. He might have to keep that news a secret until his dying days.

Erik grabbed Kristen's car keys hanging by the front door and stepped out into the bright morning light. Unlocking her rusty Toyota Camry, he settled into the driver's seat and left campus.

Though his parents didn't live far away, Erik rarely visited. The Southern Florida State University was a far cry from a suitcase school, so why leave Rachael or the eclectic activities available on campus to spend a dull weekend at home?

Yet as Erik drove down the backstreets leading out of campus, he couldn't stop a chill from seeping down his spine.

An unsettling silence pervaded in the absence of street noise and movement. It was creepy being the only moving car on the road. He turned on the old car radio to fill the silence, scanning station after station, but picked up only static.

And things didn't improve when he left campus. Heading south from the university campus in Miami Springs toward his parents' townhouse in Fountainbleau, Erik felt fortunate his parents lived in the suburbs so he could skirt most of Miami's notorious traffic issues. Still, the expressway was clogged with stalled cars and motorists stranded on their evening commutes. Which made Erik question–just how widespread were the upgrade's effects?

Was the devastation more profound than he originally suspected? Had 7G decimated the whole city? The state? The nation?

A single thought pressed him to continue weaving through the maze of stationary cars choking the expressway: it can't be everywhere. It had to have its limits. There must be some survivors. Perhaps his parents were among those spared.

Tired of inching his way through the congestion, Erik got off a few exits early and took the back roads the rest of the way home. Inside his chest, his heart sank as he passed one silent strip mall after another, the familiar sights of home transformed into an eerie ghost town. Even this close to his parents' home, not a single car crept along the road. Still, Erik kept driving, ignoring the red lights, and hoping he was wrong. That somewhere he'd find a survivor.

Suddenly, the engine chugged. Erik stepped harder on the gas pedal, but the Camry refused to accelerate. The car rolled to a slow stop in the middle of the intersection.

"I don't believe this!" Erik cursed under his breath as he pounded his fist on the center console. Then he remembered something. He glanced at the dashboard, already certain of the reason.

Sure enough, the fuel gauge's red needle cocked strongly to the left, deep below the E.

Chapter Twenty-Seven

"What a cheapskate!" Erik grumbled as he shifted the Camry into park and tripped out the driver's side.

It shouldn't surprise you. The voice of Erik's conscience filled his head. Why did it have to be so annoyingly right? How many times had he borrowed Kristen's car, only to have to fill up her tank as well?

Still, you can't be too mad at your sister, his conscience continued. She's dead.

Erik frowned. "Thanks for reminding me."

Sullenly, he peered down the street in each direction, wondering which way to head. He remembered passing a gas station about a mile back. But his parents' place wasn't much farther up the road. Might as well go the rest of the way on foot, he decided.

And what about her car? You're not gonna leave it here in the middle of the road?

"Why not?" Erik shrugged. His parents had purposefully bought her a beater for grad school. Even though they could've afforded one a little less used, they reasoned she shouldn't park something nice on the street. Shutting the door, Erik took one last look at the rusty old Camry and trudged onward, his heart filled with guilt and regret.

At least he should have plenty of time to think about how to tell his parents about Kristen, Rachael, and Lucas on the way to their townhouse. If they were even there.

If they were still alive.

There was nothing he could do about that now–not until he knew for sure.

Erik tramped down the sidewalk, his eyes trained on his feet. He passed housing developments, shopping centers, and community parks–all unnervingly quiet. He continued past the long canals running alongside the streets, constructed to improve drainage in this swampy area of South Florida near the Everglades. Suddenly Erik stopped, detecting a hint of movement in the still, brown water.

Holding his breath with heightened anticipation, Erik blinked again, anxious to find someone else alive in the midst of this apocalypse. A round, golden eye with a black, slit-like pupil protruded above the water. It studied him cautiously, perhaps hungrily for a moment, before sinking below the murky surface.

Erik exhaled deeply. It was only a gator.

And there were lots of those around here. In fact, all the townhouse complexes were gated communities now–not as added security from burglars, but from the gators themselves. Over the years, there had been too many reports of alligators swimming in pools and of residents losing small pets. The neighborhoods took action and decided to seal themselves off from uninvited guests.

An uneventful quarter mile later, Erik spotted the sign reading FOUNTAIN VIEW. With its sparklingly clear pool and Jacuzzi located on the 9th green of the Fountainbleau Municipal Golf Course, Erik admitted the Fountain View was a pretty nice place...if you liked that retirement-community-sort-of-feel.

Only today, it was dreadfully silent.

He looked through the gate, scanning the complex for signs of life. Except for the occasional bird flying overhead, he found none. Cars stood parked in several stalls, many with bodies inside.

A lump formed in Erik's throat as he keyed in the code by the front gate, hoping it hadn't changed since the summer. Luckily, the front gate swung open on creaking hinges, wide enough for a car to pass through. His stomach felt like a rock as he walked down the paved path to his parents' unit, number 203.

Erik crept up the two steps to their concrete porch and stood in front of the door, staring blankly at the brass doorknocker engraved with the name WEBER. They weren't expecting him. It wasn't like he could've called since he left his DOTS and MUDE in the dorm. Not that it mattered. Either they were here or they weren't. Erik almost hoped for the latter.

He knocked on the door, mostly because this place still didn't feel like home. Not to him, at least. After he graduated high school, his parents chose to downsize, moving into the Fountain View's townhouse community a few streets away from their old rambler. Sure, Erik had a room to himself, but it wasn't the same.

After waiting half a minute, he banged on the door again. As he suspected, there was no answer.

Just go in already.

Erik blew the hair from his eyes and cracked the door, peeking inside. "Mom? Dad?" he called, his voice cracking on each word. With bated breath, he stepped over the threshold, letting his eyes adjust to the relative darkness inside as the smell of taco meat filled his nostrils. Erik's stomach immediately flipped upside down as he tiptoed past the matching recliners sitting empty in the family room. When he entered the kitchen, he discovered the source of the smell. His mom's soft-shelled tacos piled with toppings sat half-eaten on their plates. And his parents' bodies lay face down on the floor in pools of blood that stained the Spanish tiles.

Clamping his hand over his mouth, Erik raced out of the room. Grabbing his parents' Cadillac keys off the granite countertop, he tottered outside, gasping for a decent breath. The bright sun beat upon his face, causing his head to pound unbearably, his heart stricken with grief.

So what should he do now? Where should he go when everyone he knew was dead?

He leaned his head against his parents' Cadillac, letting the hot metal scorch his forehead. Maybe the physical pain would snap him back to his senses. Though after a few seconds, Erik lifted his head again. It hadn't helped–but man, it was hot. Wincing, he put his palm to his forehead, dulling the pain, when he spotted his neighbor's ruby red Porsche parked in the adjacent spot.

Erik eyed the Porsche, his parents' keys growing heavy between his fingers.

Don't do it, his conscience warned.

Ignoring the remark, Erik dropped the Cadillac keys in his pocket and stepped toward the sports car. He ran his fingers along its smooth, shiny surface–freshly waxed, no doubt, knowing the guy's penchant for car maintenance. He glanced in the driver's side window. The keys sat on the dash, calling to him.

But there was one problem: his neighbor, Ed Watson, was still in the car, too.

How can you be so cold and heartless? Erik's conscience whined. Have you become immune to death?

Erik opened the car door and knelt down to examine Ed. Sure enough, his eyes and ears looked like the others he'd encountered.

I can't believe you're gonna steal his car.

"It's not like he needs it anymore." Not like he ever needed it in the first place. It was one of those impulsive, mid-life crisis purchases he made after his wife left him for some guy at her office.

Erik snatched the keychain off the dash and stuck a key in the ignition. Turning it one click, a broad smile spread across his face. The gas tank was full.

It's still stealing.

"I'm just borrowing it," Erik snapped as he slid Ed's body out the driver's side door. Grunting, he dragged the corpse up the curb and set it down beneath the blooming birds of paradise. Then he slipped back into the car, glad his conscience had shut up for a while. Maybe it was too appalled to think of another rebuttal.

Erik started the car, the engine roaring to life. Eager to escape this scene of death, he shifted into reverse and sped out of the stall. "I can always bring it back," Erik muttered unconvincingly as he exited the complex and took off down the road, leaving Fountainbleau. Though where he was headed, he had no idea.

Chapter Twenty-Eight

Command and Control Room, U.S.S. Siren

Even if she could make it to the top egress chamber to escape in time, Alyssa knew this was not going to be easy.

Without another moment to second-guess her action, Alyssa bolted from the Command and Control Room, back through the sloping main corridor to midship. En route, she encountered a leak in one of the pipes. Ice-cold seawater rushed in, like a firefighter's hose aimed at a raging inferno. Had they already sank to crush depth? she wondered.

Normally the crew tended leaks immediately, preventing damage to the structural stability of the submarine. However, stability was the least of her concerns now.

Blocking her face with her arms, she bulldozed her way through the torrent of incoming water. Freezing jets forcefully knocked her off her feet, blasting her face and drenching her clothes and hair. Shivering, Alyssa squeezed her eyes shut and crawled across the floor. Groping for supports, she fought against the icy surge.

Bruised and utterly soaked, she struggled past the leak toward the metal grated stairs leading to the escape hatch. Mopping the wet strands of hair that clung to her face in disheveled clumps, she glanced at the signage to confirm the location of the egress chamber. Any incorrect detours would only waste precious time.

Time in which the submarine could descend too deep for her to escape alive.

She ran up the ladder, her legs burning with the speed of her climb. Her thoughts raced, reliving the escape training at the Naval Submarine School New London in Groton, Connecticut. Terms and procedures flooded her mind. Months ago, she'd learned the history of escape procedures and been trained in the use of the equipment, but the facts quickly grew garbled in her perilous state.

The Sub School's training tower simulated the extreme pressures one would encounter when escaping a disabled submarine in the dark, deep ocean. The submariner volunteers each donned a revised model of the British Royal Navy's MK-10 Submarine Escape Immersion Equipment (What had they called it? she wondered. Oh, yeah–an SEIE): a thermally protected outfit resembling the spacesuits NASA's Apollo 11 astronauts wore on the moon–only in neon orange for enhanced visibility at sea.

Theoretically, the U.S. Navy's new MK-12 suits should enable her to escape the Siren, providing adequate protection as she ascended to the surface to wait for rescue. Yet two problems would undoubtedly impede the success of her plan...

The first: these suits worked successfully only at depths of less than 600 feet. She would have to get one on quickly before the sub sank too deep.

And the second: Alyssa had never put one on by herself before.

Sure, in Sub School it made sense that the fellow recruits assisted each other in donning these enormous SEIE suits.

Her instructors reasoned there would be several submariners attempting to escape together.

Never a single survivor.

Wrenching open the dry storage door, Alyssa tugged on the bright orange, protective garment, cursing as it got stuck on the lip of the compartment. Every passing second was a wasted one. She imagined a giant second hand ticking loudly inside her brain, like the antique grandfather clock in her hallway back home, alerting her to the dangerous passage of time. Biting her lip, Alyssa tugged again until it gave free.

Her clothes still dripping wet, she assembled the suit on the grated floor, stepping her running shoes through the leg holes and into the attached boots. Then she pulled the bulky ensemble upward, forcing her arms into the appropriate spots and her fingers into the built-in gloves. Her cold, wet clothes clung to her appendages, hindering every movement. Bending over, she reached for the zipper head and yanked on it, sealing her inside up to her chin. Already she felt encased in a form-fitting, day-glow orange sleeping bag from neck to toe. As protected as one could get for the upcoming transit to the surface.

If she weren't already chilled to the core from traversing the leak.

Finally, Alyssa pulled the wet suit fabric down over her face, covering her last remaining exposed flesh with the breathing apparatus and face shield. She felt suddenly nauseous from inhaling canister air mixed with the characteristic reek of neoprene.

Hopefully this inner thermal liner would combat the impending cold as she rose to the surface, as her instructors had assured her.

Hopefully the sub hadn't gone too deep.

Alyssa's teeth began to chatter–more from fear than cold, perhaps–as she squeezed through the watertight hatch and entered the rescue chamber. The metal cylinder enclosure was large enough to hold three escaping submariners simultaneously when cramped together. Alone, Alyssa fit easily inside. She glanced around the room, turning her entire body to search for the triggering mechanism to activate the top egress hatch. After spinning almost 180 degrees on her booted feet, Alyssa located the ball-peen hammer. Wrapping her gloved hand around its shaft, she tapped on the inside, initiating the flow of water, then waited.

She wasn't sure how long this process should take.

She wasn't sure of the Siren's current depth,

But she was certain of one thing…this was her only hope of reaching the surface.

Alive.

Chapter Twenty-Nine

A cascade of ice-cold water–frigid like glacial meltwater feeding an alpine stream–blasted in through the top of the chamber, spraying her entire body as if she bravely stood at the base of a thundering waterfall. Bracing her arms against the walls, the water continued to pound against her as it filled the floor of the chamber, squeezing her within its icy grasp. Alyssa felt her boots pinch against her calves with incredible strength and chill despite the thermal protection of the MK-12 suit.

She couldn't imagine how trapped submariners escaped from wrecks in the past, using merely an older rescue model called the Steinke Hood. It provided only head and neck protection. No thermal layer. No one-man life raft. Nothing.

Of course, they wouldn't have been able to attempt an escape from this depth, either. Silently, she thanked technological advancements, without which she would certainly have died today. Then Alyssa shuddered, her skin turning clammy–partly from the cold and partly from realizing her destiny was not guaranteed. Why jinx her escape now?

Think, Alyssa, think. What was it her instructors had mentioned so many months ago? Something about taking 90 seconds for the chamber to fill at a depth of 600 feet below the surface. Why hadn't she remembered that earlier? She chastised herself for not counting, "One-Mississippi, Two-Mississippi," from the start as an estimate of her current depth. Now it was too late.

The water level inched upward, compressing her MK-12 Escape Suit tightly against her thighs and augmenting the seeping chill that already pervaded her body, drenched from the leak. Through chattering teeth, Alyssa's breaths came out short and shallow. Panicked. Breathe. Just breathe, she coached herself. It was imperative she stop hyperventilating if she were to survive the ascent.

Alyssa forced herself to focus on the details from the training tower where she tested a similar escape suit. But her brain felt fuzzy—perhaps a natural side effect from witnessing so much death.

I feel like I'm never going to see you again. Her mother's somber words echoed in her head as the water level rose past her neck, clutching her throat in its chilling grip. She desperately tried to ignore the numbness in her appendages, the weight of the water squeezing every inch of her body. She gasped in pain, as if a boa constrictor wrapped her tightly in its coils, taking advantage of every exhalation to tighten its grip further, slowly wringing the life from her.

Alyssa bit her lip, keeping the tears at bay. She assured her mother she'd return safely; she couldn't fall back on that promise now, not when she was so close to escaping. So what else had she learned during training? Something about screaming to prevent one's lungs from being crushed by the intense pressure at excessive depths? Between the dizzying atrocities she witnessed on board and the water gushing against her helmet's face shield, it was hard to remember clearly. Alyssa's head pounded as she strained to keep it upright against the deafening roar of water pouring in from the outside.

She did recall reading about escaping submariners shouting, "I FEEL FINE!" And how expelling forceful breaths would prevent their lungs from collapsing as they ascended the vertical tower of cold, pressurized water. Alyssa heeded this warning and began to scream–though she couldn't perceive her own voice over the roaring flow of water streaming upon her face shield, rattling every inch of her skull.

Soon the water level inched above her face, disrupting the deafening spray. Now that her body was squeezed numb and the roar of the pouring water had subsided, Alyssa felt she could refocus her energies once more. Between screams, an eerie sense of calm filled the air of her face shield. She could actually hear her own words repeated again and again, "I FEEL FINE!"

Though she no longer believed them.

A few seconds after the water level passed over her head, the top egress hatch suddenly unlatched with a loud click.

This was it. There was no looking back.

Mid-scream, the door flew open. Alyssa rocketed upward as the buoyant suit shot her toward the surface. A flurry of bubbles zoomed past her face, obscuring her view of the intense blackness of the deep sea. As her body succumbed to the extreme cold and pressure, it decreased blood flow to her extremities. Alyssa felt her fingertips and toes grow numb, her body hypothermic.

For long minutes, Alyssa screamed as she ascended, wishing an end to the chilling pain. Eventually, her throat grew raw and hoarse, her voice weary with exhaustion. How much farther to the surface? She glanced upward, but detected no signs of light penetrating to this depth. Probably a few hundred feet to go.

Alyssa wasn't sure she would make it in time.

Images of death flooded her mind, like a dam rupturing after heavy spring rains. Carly Zapelli who she'd known from the beginning of training…her berthmate, Rosemary Dela Cruz…Medical Officer Knolls and his dashed dreams of spending quality time with his kids…the faces of so many crewmembers she'd barely known…

And Justin.

Filled with despair, Alyssa's throat tightened as a new wave of emotion broke upon her.

Choked with fear, her cries (or lies about feeling fine) transformed into a desperate plea. "I DON'T WANT TO DIE!" she shouted in earnest, praying to God that she would somehow survive this ordeal.

Minutes passed. Alyssa's throat burned with each uttered word. Her lungs felt depleted. Yet the water column seemed as black as a moonless night.

This wasn't how she had planned to die.

Drowned. And alone.

Chapter Thirty

She was a swimmer, for God's sake. She could do this.

Squeezing the tears from her eyes, she willed herself to focus strictly on the ascent. By pressing her arms tightly against her sides, she streamlined her body into a torpedo shape, cutting through the icy, midnight water. She kicked her boots robotically: one, two, one, two.

In Varsity swim practices, this technique helped her concentrate on the mechanics of her stroke as one arm broke the surface to reach deep below, pulling downward in a serpentine motion. Her cupped hand seized new water, propelling her forward. Then it exited past her hip as the other arm initiated its stroke sequence. The rhythmic ritual allowed her to ignore the fatiguing burn building in her arms and shoulders...and fueled her desire to swim faster than her competitors.

Closing her eyes, Alyssa suppressed the pain in her heaving chest and resisted the desire to claw at her parched throat. And–with as much strength as she could muster–continued to scream.

When she dared to open her eyes again, the water appeared lighter, as if a few faint rays of light had permeated its depths. Alyssa's mood similarly brightened. She was getting closer. C'mon, Alyssa, you can do this. You promised Mom, she repeated in her mind as she persisted upward.

Her screams of desperation ached inside her parched throat with every uttered word, her voice no more than a forced whisper. Her eyes fluttered upward again, hopeful for some clue as to the distance remaining. Alyssa's heart beat rapidly as she spotted flickers of moonlight dancing upon the ocean waves above.

Light! How many long months had passed since she'd last seen natural light? Losing track of the normal passage of time in her underwater world of perpetual artificial light and 18-hour days, Alyssa had longed for the warmth of the sun's rays to beat upon face. A chance to bask in the sun's bright beams or gaze upon the moon's glow on a cloudless night.

She couldn't give up now.

A wide smile formed upon her face. One that quickly disappeared as panic engulfed her...

Suddenly, she couldn't breathe.

Alyssa gasped for air, but found none in her depleted oxygen supply. So the Siren must've sunk below 600 feet when the top egress opened, she figured. It was the only explanation for her Submarine Escape Immersion Equipment failing her now.

Filling her mouth with the illusion of a breath, Alyssa puffed out her cheeks and clamped her lips shut. Her head spun, dizzy from lack of oxygen.

Alyssa realized this was The End. She wasn't going to survive.

How ironic for her to perish within sight of the surface.

"Almost. There," her voice croaked as she frantically clawed the water, exhausting the remains of her energy in a burst of powerful kicks. Her arms reached for the air. Her legs fought the resistance of the suit's folds of fabric as her feet battled the weight of the attached boots. Her lungs burned like wildfires scorching the drought-stricken wilderness of her searing throat.

With one last desperate stroke, Alyssa achieved the impossible. Her head broke the surface, amidst churning wave crests. Alyssa ripped off the face shield and breathing apparatus, choking as fresh air entered her oxygen-deficient lungs. She treaded water momentarily to tug the ripcord from the outer compartment of her suit. Instantly, a gas-inflated life raft ballooned beneath her. Fighting exhaustion, she bobbed with the rise and fall of the sea. The homing beacon automatically activated, blinking bright yellow against the inky sea to alert others to her presence.

Alyssa reclined against the inflated side of the raft while ghostly whitecaps rocked her back and forth. She reminded herself to stay vigilant. She flexed her fingers and toes, hoping to return the flow of blood to her extremities.

It wasn't over yet.

Subconsciously, her thoughts returned to her training. The survival techniques she'd learned but never expected to ever use. The physical agony and mental anguish she'd endured, preparing her for this moment. The camaraderie engrained in the masses to work together as a single unit.

Her unit she'd left behind–dead in the deep.

Images of crewmates' faces whipped through her mind at an incredible rate. The overwhelming pangs of loss sent her brain cartwheeling out of control. Alyssa bit her lip, hugging herself as her body shook with convulsive tears. She clutched her throat, gasping for a decent breath. She squeezed her fingers, unable to gain sensation. And she cried and cried until no tears remained.

Utterly exhausted, she collapsed in the raft. The world around her soon faded into blackness like the abysmal depths of water from which she had just escaped.

Chapter Thirty-One

South Miami, Florida

What's the point in continuing? Erik Weber mused as he drove south, through one ghost town after another.

Honestly. Everyone he knew and loved is gone. So why not him, too?

Erik drove on, his senses dull and unresponsive. There was nothing left to live for. He could literally drive this car (stolen car, his conscience reminded him) straight off a bridge and no one would ever know. Or care.

But then an image of Rachael flashed through his muddled mind. Memories of happier times broke through the shadowy cloud of despair, filling his soul. He envisioned the animated and vivacious face of the girl he fell in love with. The endearing smile she saved especially for him. The smell of her hair when he held her close. The warmth of her hand entwined with his.

Erik released a heavy sigh. He could never apologize for the misunderstanding about her cousin, Jamie. Never. And he could go mad dwelling on that fact for the remainder of his days, however short and pathetic they might be.

Rachael was gone. Kristen, his parents, and Lucas, too. And there was nothing he could do to bring them back. Erik's heart felt hollow and empty, brimming with despair.

But you're not dead. Not yet, at least.

True, the thought of taking his own life tempted Erik. It would bring an end to the heartache. And a chance to reunite with his lost ones once more.

Only Rachael would never forgive you.

Erik nodded. She sacrificed her life to save his, hadn't she? Granted, she might not have consciously made that sacrifice, but it'd happened nonetheless. The only way he could honor her memory now, was to move on. Forge a new existence out of nothing.

An urgent sense of responsibility lifted his spirits. He wasn't sure how he'd do it, but somehow he'd persist. He owed her that much. He owed all of them that much.

Turning off the highway, Erik meandered aimlessly down one street after another, eventually finding himself on a residential boulevard lined with tall palm trees. His eyes bulged as he gazed upon the luxury homes with freshly manicured lawns, white stucco exteriors and red tile roofs. Each had expensive cars parked in their three-car garages, in-ground swimming pools, and boats docked along private canal slips in the backyards. Probably all vacant now, he thought grimly.

He'd always dreamed of living in a place like this someday, like his parents' friends, the Goldmans. The Goldmans had owned a gorgeous home on Biscayne Bay in the upscale community of Gables by the Sea. Erik had spent most childhood weekends there, swimming in their pool and sailing on their private yacht, the Golden Sunrise. They sold the place during the housing boom and made a small fortune.

Then they moved into a classy townhouse and bought a new boat to store at a slip in Miami.

Erik had loved that old yacht. He remembered sitting in the bow of the Golden Sunrise with Kristen, eating tuna fish sandwiches and sugar cookies as they dangled their bare feet over the side, the sea spray tickling their toes. But over the years, those family outings became more and more infrequent. Erik and Kristen often made excuses to hang out with friends instead of joining their parents and the Goldmans for an afternoon at sea. As a teenager, Erik found it frustrating to leave the speed of his travel to the whim of the wind. In fact, he'd only been out on their new boat, the Golden Sunset, a couple of times.

Yet his parents begged him to come back once this semester. He'd even considered inviting Rachael; she would've loved getting away from campus to spend a few hours out on the water. Only he'd hesitated in making such a big step prematurely. Almost as if the simple act of meeting his parents would bump their relationship up a notch from "casual" to "serious." And he didn't want to risk losing her over that.

Except now you've lost her altogether. Without ever having the chance to…

Suddenly Erik slammed on the brakes. The Porsche skidded to a halt. In an instant, he knew what he must do. Turning the car around he sped up the street, back toward Miami. For the first time since this nightmare began, he was certain of the future.

If he could get out of the city in time.

Chapter Thirty-Two

Three miles off the coast of Miami

The rocking of the lifeboat woke Alyssa Kensington. Not a soothing lullaby sort of awakening, but a jolt into her hellish reality of being stranded. Alone. In the middle of God-knows-where.

Somehow, against the odds, she had survived. How and why, she didn't know.

She bolted upright. The froth from the whitecaps sprayed her face with its harsh sting, jarring Alyssa to her senses. Wispy clouds streaked the bright sky, like artists' brushstrokes across a fresh canvas. Squinting, her eyes adjusted to the sunlight while she tried to make sense of the horrors she'd witnessed.

The Siren's dead crew and officers. Her friend, Carly Zapelli. Medical Officer Knolls.

And Justin.

A single tear rolled down her cheek. Alyssa steeled her resolve, knowing this wasn't the time for grieving. Her mother would be waiting at home, frantic with worry that Alyssa had also perished in the sunken ship. "I've gotta get back," she told herself in a raspy voice, hoarse from screaming upon her ascent.

But how?

All around her was open water. Miles and miles of nothing but blue.

As she scanned the horizon, hopeful for a sign of land, her eyes rested on the yellow light attached to her suit. It'd been blinking all night. So where was the Coast Guard? Or the airlift medevac? They should've been here by now. Surely they couldn't miss spotting her in this day-glow orange suit and life raft.

Still, she couldn't sit around and wait forever. She thought back to the chart of the Florida coast. The chart lying under Justin's inert body, its corner soaked with blood. His blood.

Blinking back the tears, she tried to focus on the bathymetric chart itself. She recalled the Gulf Stream hugging the tip of the Florida coast. It could easily push her out of reach of shore.

If it hadn't already done so.

"For the love of God," Alyssa moaned, staring up at the sky. "How long have I been waiting?"

Yet the sky lay eerily quiet in the bright morning light. No chopping blades. No sounds of jet engines slicing across the crisp blue, either. And Alyssa had no measure of the time of day or her current location–not without the eye DOTS. So she'd have to rely on visuals, instead. Sun, clouds, and haze over the nearby concrete jungle of Miami. "Face it Alyssa, you're screwed."

She tried to relax and wait, but that was impossible. Her ordeal wasn't over.

At least an hour must have passed while Alyssa bobbed on the surface, deliberating over her options. She couldn't be that far from shore, could she? Had the current dragged her father out to sea? And where was the rescue boat?

She couldn't risk waiting any longer. Swallowing hard, Alyssa peered into the distance. West, she thought, judging by the sun's movement across the sky. Far away, clouds hovered above a low-lying, dark patch of…land.

Scratch that–make it LAND!

She squinted again. Between the intense sunbeams shimmering off the surface and her mental exhaustion, she wasn't certain. But when she wheeled her head around, she found only open water behind her. So it must be.

She looked back down at her orange suit. Sure, her chances of survival were increased with the thermal barrier and increased visibility of the MK-12 suit. But the Gulf Stream was a warm current and her muscles would generate heat during exercise. Not to mention, the suit was stinking heavy. She thought back to her struggle to the surface, battling the bulky folds of fabric that billowed in the water as she swam upward. She had to lose it.

Then could she make it? If she swam for it?

Alyssa noticed a cord running around the circumference of the raft. She yanked it free of its loops and secured it around her waist. She stripped off the SEIE suit, her work uniform underneath, and her running shoes. Standing in her skivvies, she contemplated her next step. It's either this or wait some more, she reminded herself.

But she'd been waiting so long already. "Too long," Alyssa decided as she tied her gear to the inside of the raft. Then she eased herself into the water and began to swim.

The first few strokes felt refreshing as she stretched out her sore arms and legs, trying to remember the last time her body sliced through cool water. Or a trail of bubbles streamed against her cheek when she exhaled. The exertion soon warmed her muscles from the inside and returned blood flow to her extremities.

But the refreshing sensation quickly faded. Alyssa's arms and legs were not just sore–they were spent. Yesterday's ordeal of battling the leak and escaping the Siren taxed her body far more than she had originally imagined. Each stroke soon became unbearable, reminding her of Coach Sparks' infamous "Red Shirt" workouts. Deep red–like the color of death. (Which, Alyssa remembered, was often how she felt after experiencing one.) With his jaw set and an intense look in his narrowed eyes, Coach Sparks would arrive early at Saturday morning swim practice wearing a red shirt flaunting the phrase I'M GONNA K YOUR A.

And that's exactly what he'd proceed to do.

Two hours and six miles later, Alyssa's arms dragged across the ground as she heaved her limp body out of the pool and staggered to the locker rooms to change. Even his mandatory second breakfast following practice couldn't cure her aching limbs. Then, after a mere day of rest, she was back at it Monday before school.

His training methods may have seemed extreme (especially when he barked at one of her teammates for having menstrual cramps, claiming anyone who got her period wasn't swimming hard enough). But Alyssa dealt with it, knowing his grueling workouts enabled her to drop her times...and win events. The thrill of competition and success sustained her through the less-than-pleasant parts of practice.

Stroke, stroke, stroke, breathe. Stroke, stroke, stroke, breathe. Alyssa quickly slipped into the familiar rhythm of arcing her arm above the surface, sending water droplets streaming from her fingertips. She rolled her shoulders to increase her reach as she dug deep with each pull.

Periodically, she'd lift her head straight out of the water to verify she maintained her course toward land.

At first, the familiar routine helped Alyssa forget. She focused on song lyrics she used to play through her head hour after hour during practice. Exciting moments of races she'd won in the last few lengths. Fond memories of hiking on mountain trails those days off from school...

School. Her friends.

Then she remembered Steve and Ellen...and reality struck.

Alyssa's face reddened from the betrayal she'd felt, learning they started going out right after her departure. It wasn't like she wanted Steve back. She just didn't want anyone else to have him. Not yet, at least. And especially not Ellen...ever. That wasn't too much to ask, was it?

Alyssa's arms shot out of the water with increased fury. How dare they!

And Justin. Just when she'd found a spot of happiness aboard the Siren. So much for the possibility of their future together. And to think her greatest concern had been getting caught!

Her feet kicked the water harder, livid at having him ripped away.

Turning her head to the side, she gasped for air above the choppy surf. Each breath burned her parched throat. Tears spilled from her eyes, mingling with the salty sea. Gulping a mouthful of water on her next breath, she coughed and stopped, treading water as she choked on flowing tears.

"ENOUGH!" she hollered hoarsely, pulling her hair by the roots. "He's gone. They're all gone." She sobbed softly, her legs alternately kicking to keep her buoyant.

Why bother? It'd be so much easier to simply give up. To freely sink below the surface, back to the place she'd been so desperate to escape.

Then she remembered her mom; Alyssa had promised to return home. She thought of Tucker, waiting for her with a wide grin and greeting her with slobbery kisses.

She squinted into the distance again. The land did appear considerably closer. Safety was within reach.

Setting her jaw, Alyssa suddenly knew what she had to do. Whatever it takes, she would survive.

The time for tears had ended.

With renewed strength, she ducked her head back in the water, her arms spinning once more. Her legs felt surprisingly tireless, churning the water in her wake. She ignored the tug of the raft bobbing behind her as she focused on her goal. She'd endured worse before, thanks to Coach Sparks.

Mom. Tucker. Mom Tucker. The words replayed in her head with every stroke. (Though occasionally Alyssa's thoughts shifted to the joy she'd derive in decking Steve Summers. Just to get him back for what he'd put her through.)

Long ago, she'd forgotten about the hunger gnawing at the inside of her stomach. The hollowness she felt, exacerbated by physical exertion. But one pressing concern was impossible to ignore.

Thirst.

The salt water seemed to suck all reserves from her body. It was tempting-so very tempting-to open her mouth and take one little sip. Surrounding her was a bounty of liquid, waiting to quench her need. Biting her lip, Alyssa willed herself to concentrate on the efficiency of each stroke to conserve her energy.

She recalled the naval lore of shipwrecks and sailors stranded at sea. In desperation, some drank the seawater, only to succumb to the deliria that followed. Tempted by mirages of distant islands, they swam off. Through schools of circling sharks.

Never to be seen again.

Instead, Alyssa swallowed hard, gaining minute relief from the tiny amount of spittle collecting in her mouth. It would have to suffice for now.

Soon, however, Alyssa concluded this agony was indeed worse than any of Coach Sparks' kick-butt Red Shirt practices. More painful than the grueling hours of swimming in T-shirts, nylons, and tennis shoes to strengthen her muscles by increasing her drag. She raised her head above the waves again. Thank God the land seemed closer yet.

She pressed on, trying to forget her insufferable thirst. The stranded sailors who swam away. And the sharks.

Alyssa's brain shut down, entering automaton mode. Her fatigued body grasped the water, minute after grueling minute as land came clearly into sight.

At last, the spilling waves pushed Alyssa toward shore, washing her up on the beach. The raft dragged behind, tumbling in the surf. Alyssa stumbled as another wave broke upon her and threw her to her knees. Spray and sand from the breaking waves splattered her weary face. Wiping her eyes, she crawled toward the raft, flipping it over to wash the sand from her attached clothes.

Her legs like limp noodles, Alyssa tripped in the surf. She hauled the raft up the sloping beach, like scaling a cliff in her exhausted state.

Land.

All thoughts of thirst, fatigue, and hunger fled her mind as she sank to her knees in the sand, feeling the grit of terra firma beneath her toes. She grabbed handfuls of packed sand, proving it wasn't a mirage that eluded her to a false sense of security when death loomed near.

The sand felt real. Alyssa heaved a deep breath, finally allowing herself a smile. The smell of brine lingered in the air. Brine and…something else. Alyssa couldn't put her finger on it, but it didn't really matter.

She had made it. She had survived.

Though deep down she knew there was little time to rejoice. Not if she were to help raise the Siren from its sunken depths.

Chapter Thirty-Three

Once on dry sand, Alyssa untied the cord from her waist, freeing herself at last from the raft. She didn't care if people saw her in dripping underwear while she untied her clothes and jammed her unresponsive limbs back into the wet Navy work uniform and running shoes. In fact, she didn't see anyone around. Might as well leave the raft and SEIE suit here, she figured. It didn't seem like anyone would notice.

Now to get help. Forgetting her oppressive thirst, Alyssa surveyed her surroundings, trying to determine which way to head. Things would've been so much easier with her eye DOTS; she'd have instant access to a wealth of contact information. Of course, with them in she wouldn't have had to swim to shore, either. Not when she could've easily notified Search and Rescue of her precise location.

Wetting her parched lips, Alyssa headed down the seemingly deserted beach. Having spent the last two months away from civilization, it took her a moment to realize that even the nearby street sounded quiet.

Oddly quiet.

In fact, the only noise she perceived over her squishy wet shoes and the waves washing up the beach was the crying flock of herring gulls, circling a couple of distant, dark mounds.

So where is everybody? Alyssa wondered, perplexed by the absence of late-season beachgoers on this calm, clear day. She straggled up the sand to the road, finding a single car parked on the shoulder. Alyssa peered inside, rapping her knuckles on the window, but received no response. Hair spilling across her face, the driver's head slumped against the steering wheel. Probably drunk, Alyssa assumed.

Alyssa spun her head, looking for someone else to ask. Still, there was no one around. So she ambled along the shoulder, in the direction of the squawking gulls. There appeared to be a parking lot down a ways, near the beach entrance. Perhaps she could find someone to place a call for her. When she was a kid, it wouldn't have been a problem; public phones were generally accessible. But those had vanished entirely with the advent of the DOTS.

Glancing back to sea, Alyssa noticed there weren't any swimmers in the water, either. Only a sleek, silvery dorsal fin cutting through the surf. Had the lifeguards closed the beaches because of the sharks? Then how had Alyssa made it out of the water safely?

A shiver ran down her spine, chilling her with the thought of coming so far only to perish within feet of land. Her hands cupped her elbows, warding off the fear.

Strangely enough, the whole time she'd been walking, not a single car passed for Alyssa to flag down for help. She squinted into the bright sun. Not one plane had taken off or landed, either.

Why is that?

She continued, pondering the unsettling quiet surrounding her. Then it dawned on her: something was wrong.

Terribly, horribly, dreadfully wrong.

Those heaps on the beach…they weren't piles of trash as she'd initially believed, were they? As she neared the maddening cries of the gulls, the dark masses began to take on a sickeningly familiar form. Alyssa tiptoed closer, praying she was mistaken.

She wasn't.

Scrunching up her nose, Alyssa suddenly recognized the odor she had difficulty identifying earlier. It was the smell of death. And decay.

Alyssa froze. In front of her, unmistakable now, lay two human corpses strewn across the sand. A gull perched on top of one man's face, picking at an empty eye socket with its bill.

She swallowed hard, unable to control the surge of bile up her esophagus. Alyssa doubled over, clutching the sand for support. The last remaining fluids inside her empty stomach erupted out her mouth, soon followed by a set of dry heaves. What little strength and sustenance had remained following her harrowing escape now vacated Alyssa's body, leaving her insides raked with torment.

Alyssa's mind reeled as she staggered past the screeching gulls and the bloated bodies on the beach. Overhead, palm trees circled at a dizzying rate, threatening to collapse upon her. What type of destructive force caused such widespread destruction and devastation, essentially annihilating an entire population, both above and below the sea? Some type of biological weapon? Or a terrorist attack?

It didn't make sense.

Alyssa tried to steady herself. Her feet weighed like dragging anchors with every step. No tears remained for these strangers. Those had dried up long ago, far out at sea.

Shaking uncontrollably, she wrapped her arms around her chest, urging herself to press forward. She tried to block out the image of Justin's bloodstained face keeled over bathymetric chart on the light table. Or Carly Zapelli sprawled across the grated metal floor. Why did these bodies on the beach have bloody ears and eyes like her crewmates? And why was she spared when so many others perished?

What could have possibly happened?

Dehydrated, Alyssa's head pounded like a bass drum, making it difficult to think clearly, much less generate a logical explanation. The scenery around her blurred as she stumbled past cars, their passengers slumped against the windows and seats inside. Unable to take another step, she collapsed in the middle of the street, one hand clutching her burning throat. She laid her cheek against the hot pavement, feeling the asphalt dig into her skin. Utterly exhausted, her eyelids sagged. Her muscles grew unresponsive as they melted into the road.

So this was it? Had Alyssa escaped the Siren only to perish in this avenue of death?

Before Alyssa could ponder the irony of that question, she heard the sound of tires gripping the road. With tremendous effort, she fluttered open her eyes. A flurry of movement in the distance caught her attention as a red sports car skidded around the corner.

Alyssa was too weary to register surprise. But in the back of her mind, one thought persisted: Get help. Even if she could've summoned the energy to move out of the way, it would've been too late. So with her last remaining ounce of effort, Alyssa stretched one weakened arm in the air, beckoning for help.

No cry escaped her parched lips as the car careened closer.

Chapter Thirty-Four

Miami Beach

In the red Porsche, Erik Weber stepped on the gas. The harbor was only a few miles away. It was time to get out of Miami — now. He planned to take the Goldman's boat, certain he'd recognize it. Erik shuddered at the thought of what he might have to do with their bodies if he found the boat occupied. Moving Ed Watson from the car to the curb was one thing, but tossing his family friends' bodies overboard? He simply couldn't. So if that were the case, he'd have to select an unoccupied boat instead.

Then Erik spotted something lying in the middle of the road.

"Holy hell! What is that?" he screamed.

At first it resembled a flock of buzzards scavenging a corpse, ready to scatter at the approaching vehicle. But it was too narrow. Like a hand. A human hand that...moved? Erik blinked, just to be sure. Indeed, he detected five fingers, spreading apart, beckoning.

Someone's alive!

Erik slammed on the brakes. The car swerved as it screeched to a halt, leaving wide black ribbons of rubber on the hot pavement.

Throwing the Porsche into park, Erik leapt out of the driver's seat, leaving the door wide open.

"Are you okay?" he asked, kneeling beside the person. He pushed her short, disheveled brown hair from her face. She looks about my age, he thought. So what was she doing here? Alone?

And alive?

Her hazel eyes didn't register on his face; her lips barely moved. Erik placed his hand upon her forehead, burning to his touch. Though he knew nothing about this person, he felt a sudden compulsion to get her out of here and bring her somewhere safe.

Erik swept her up in his arms, lifting her into the car. She tossed fitfully, mumbling a few garbled words that sounded like, "Trapped...egress...Justin." He leaned his left ear closer to her lips, but caught nothing more as she slipped into unconsciousness.

As Erik buckled her into the passenger seat, he noticed her name reading KENSINGTON and the insignia on her uniform. A set of dog tags slipped out of her shirt as her head rolled against the seat belt.

Unbelievable. A smug smile crossed Erik's face. Sailing would be so much easier with two. Especially with someone like her.

If only he could revive her.

Chapter Thirty-Five

"Alyssa? Alyssa Kensington?"

A pleasant voice broke through her subconscious. It was Justin calling her, waking her from a horrendous nightmare in Quarantine. Only the voice sounded off…and unfamiliar.

Alyssa flitted her eyes, startled by the brilliance. The sub was never this brightly lit. How long had she been sleeping? Was her stint in Quarantine finished? And why did her body feel so depleted?

"I didn't think I should leave you at first," said the congenial voice again, "but you were out for a while. So I brought you some food. Thought you might be hungry."

She turned toward the voice, seeking comfort and reassurance in Justin's warm brown eyes, gazing upon her inside the confines of the Quarantine Room.

Instead, she met a pair of weary gray ones, bloodshot from exhaustion and stress. Blinking in confusion, she focused on the foreign eyes and the sandy blonde hair falling in waves across a rosy face, then to the tall palm trees towering overhead.

Suddenly, Alyssa bolted upright. This was no nightmare. Vivid memories rushed through her mind: of finding her dead crewmates in a sinking sub, of escaping through the black void of the ocean, and of enduring an agonizing swim to shore...only to encounter more death.

What was she doing, sitting here wasting time? Why hadn't she made him get help? The Navy or the Coast Guard could've already deployed a rescue team to raise the Siren. Her mouth moved too quickly to form coherent words as her frantic eyes searched those of the stranger before her.

"Oh. Sorry." He must've noticed her confusion and panic. "My name's Erik. Erik Weber. I didn't get a chance to introduce myself before you passed out. Here," he said, holding up a box of powdered doughnuts and a half-gallon of orange juice, "go ahead."

Alyssa opened her mouth to speak, then shut it again. Strangely, she couldn't take her eyes off the food. She knew should contact the authorities immediately. Or at least have Erik (that was his name, right?) use his DOTS to place the call for her. But her hollow stomach protested. How long had it been since her last meal? Plus her throat burned...and the acrid taste of bile still lingered in her mouth.

"Go ahead. It's yours," Erik repeated, handing her the food.

Eat fast...then get help, she decided, smiling in appreciation. She snatched the bottle of orange juice from him and twisted the cap, downing its contents in a single gulp. Wiping her mouth on her sleeve, her eyes fell onto the unopened box of doughnuts.

Erik peeled back the plastic wrapper and passed it to her. "So, you're in the Navy?"

Alyssa nodded, jamming half the powdered doughnut into her mouth in one bite.

"Then you know how to sail, right?"

The sugar and flour stuck like glue inside her mouth. She tried to say, "I was on a sub," but it came out more like a choked garble.

"I'll take that as a yes." His weary eyes lit up momentarily. "I was thinking we should take a sailboat. You know, as backup so we can save the gas. There's a nice one in the harbor, but it's too big for just me. I thought if we worked together–"

Alyssa swallowed hard, the food clinging to the walls of her esophagus. "What?! You're gonna steal a boat?" Her sore body tensed in shock from his statement.

"Well, it's not really stealing. My parents' friends own it." A melancholy look passed over his face. "At least, they used to."

Enough food for now. It's time to move on, Alyssa reminded herself, stuffing one more doughnut into her mouth as she stood to leave. She chewed quickly, forcing the lump down her throat. "Thanks for the food, but I've gotta get help. I need you to make a call for me."

Erik shook his head. "Can't."

"But my whole crew's still stuck down there!" Alyssa protested.

"And they're gonna stay there," he said grimly as he rose to his feet. "There's nothing you can do about it."

Alyssa's eyes widened with exasperation. How could he be so heartless? "What about my mom?! She must be worried sick. She probably thinks I'm dead, too!"

"You can't call anyone. Not anymore." Now his voice sounded steely cold. Calculated.

Fear seized Alyssa like skeletal fingers closing around her throat. She'd read about cases like this before—when a beguiling psychopath charmed his victim, luring her away from civilization before slitting her throat. She had to get away from this stranger. And fast.

Instantly, self-defense maneuvers shot forth from her memory: a swift kick to the groin, a blow to the nose, then take off screaming.

Without another word, she slammed the toe of her running shoe into his crotch and the palm of her hand thrust upward, connecting with his nose. Then she bolted toward the parking lot. Permitting herself a quick glance backward, she saw Erik swearing loudly as he doubled over in pain, one hand clutching his groin and the other the bridge of his bloody nose. Satisfied, she sprinted as fast as her legs would allow. Her heart hammered inside her chest and her pulse throbbed wildly inside her neck. All the while, she yelled for help, but her hoarse voice didn't carry far–even in the disturbing quiet that surrounded her.

Over the sounds of waves sloshing up the beach, she soon heard heavy footsteps trailing her. Obviously, her tired leg hadn't kicked him hard enough.

Heading toward the strip of hotels ahead, Alyssa tried to pick up her pace, but her body ached with each motion, her joints screeching in pain. Had she escaped from the Siren only yesterday? It seemed ages ago.

The footsteps came closer, yet she didn't dare look back as she charged for the front door of the nearest hotel. Then she felt his fingers wrap around her forearm. A high-pitched shriek escaped Alyssa's lips as he wheeled her to face him. She shouted, "Lemme alone!" hoping someone in the nearby buildings would rush to her aid. Fighting against him, Alyssa kicked madly with her free leg, her heel hitting his shinbone. Erik howled in pain, instantly releasing his grip.

Free again, she darted down the street. Almost there, she thought encouragingly, keeping her eyes trained on the welcoming hotel door. But his footsteps pounded the pavement just behind her.

Erik gasped, "Alyssa! Listen to me!" as he snatched her arm again. She thrashed wildly, trying to free herself once more. Only this time, Erik pulled her closer, securing his arms tightly around her body to restrain her. He pinned his chin against her collarbone, whispering through gritted teeth, "Everyone's gone. Look around!"

His words echoed in the unnatural stillness of the street. For a moment, Alyssa stopped struggling. Through crazed eyes, she glanced down the road and across the beach. Suddenly, she understood the reason behind the lack of noise. No cars were moving. No people, either.

What in God's name happened to Miami?

Erik locked his fingers in her hair, turning her head to look him straight in the eye. "I know it's painful to remember, but on the sub…what did you see?"

Alyssa squeezed her eyes shut. She shook her head, blocking out the horrors.

"Please, Alyssa," he implored. "Did you see them bleeding? From their eyes and ears?"

"SHUT UP!" she screamed, smothering her ears with her hands. "What's wrong with you?! Why are you doing this to me?" All she could think of were her fallen crewmates. And Justin.

But somewhere in the back of her mind, she wondered, How did he know? Slowly, reluctantly, she dropped her hands, staring at him with wide eyes.

His fingers relaxed in her hair. Softer, Erik probed, "And you? Did you have your DOTS in?"

"Of course," Alyssa snapped. "Everyone does. It's mandatory."

Erik frowned, releasing her altogether. Wiping his bloody nose on the back of his hand, he sank to the ground. His head drooped, defeated, as if searching for a new theory to explain the annihilation surrounding him.

Puzzled, Alyssa studied him for a moment. Maybe he wasn't some psychopath like she'd suspected. Maybe he was just frightened and alone...like her.

A part of her regretted hitting him in the nose. And kicking him. Twice.

Then Alyssa remembered something. "Oh. My. God," she breathed. She unbuttoned her chest pocket and pulled out the bottle of sulfacetamide drops.

She'd completely forgotten about her Pinkeye. Conjunctivitis. Whatever.

Through her muddled brain rang the voice of Medical Officer Michael Knolls, crystal clear in her ears. *The next upgrade comes into effect tomorrow. We'll get you a fresh set of gear once your quarantine is completed.*

7G.

Alyssa gasped as she stared at Erik. "You don't think...?"

Erik raised his head, looking at her bottle of prescription eye drops. "You didn't have them in, did you?"

Slowly, she shook her head. "I was sent to Quarantine. They removed them as a precaution."

"I had mine out, too," he said weakly. "And now...well...look at us."

They were the only ones standing.

It took a minute for the weight of the news to sink into Alyssa's brain.

There'd been a lot of hype over this National Conversion, promising Americans the latest encryption devices to prevent terrorist attacks and optical/audio recording capabilities for personal enjoyment, making the U.S. the pinnacle of telecommunications in the world.

So was her mother's premonition true? They would never see each other again? And what about Steve and Ellen? Suddenly, her anger over their relationship seemed decidedly trivial. She never had a chance to say goodbye to her best friend. To any of them, for that matter.

Alyssa realized with remorse that America's obsession for the fastest, most advanced, and immediate communication had ultimately led to its demise.

Glancing around the lifeless strip of hotel-lined beach, Alyssa wondered if her escape from the Siren had only condemned her to another level of hell.

Chapter Thirty-Six

"I'm still going back," Alyssa said defiantly and turned away. Even if she couldn't contact her mom, she could still drive to Virginia and on to D.C. There had to be some government official there she could contact about the sunken sub. Regardless of whether Erik was right or not, she had to see it with her own eyes.

Erik placed his hand on her wrist, stopping her. "Listen. There's nothing to go back to. Phones. T.V. Radio. Everything's gone. Everyone's gone." Quieter, he added, "I'm sorry. I thought I was it. You're the first one I found —"

" — alive," Alyssa finished for him. She knew how he felt. All too well. But that wasn't enough for her to abandon her quest. One hundred thirty-eight submariners lay dead, trapped in a metal hull on the sea floor. And they would remain there for eternity unless she did something about it. Maybe Erik's theory was flawed. Maybe the devastation was simply regional. The entire world couldn't have perished in a single night.

"How'd you figure it out? I mean, in a way it makes sense," she said as her mind pieced the evidence together. "But still. How'd you know for sure?"

"I had mine out, too. And when I went to put them back in to call 911..." Erik clamped his hand to his head, remembering the pain. "Let's just say it was pretty obvious."

Cocking one eyebrow high on her forehead, she pressed, "How so?"

Erik hung his head miserably. "The pain. In my eyes. And ear." He wiped the right side of his face, as if checking for ghostly streams of blood trickling down his cheek. "It was intense. I still can't hear on one side." He tapped his right ear, frowning. "I feel so bad for them. It must not've been a pleasant way to go."

Alyssa sank to the ground, wrapping her arms around her chest. She fell silent, staring in disbelief at the empty sky as she fought back the gory recollection of the dead crew aboard the Siren.

"You really think they're all gone?" she whispered, choking on the gravity of each word.

Erik sighed as he sat down next to her. "Not everyone, of course. I'm sure there's still pockets of survivors scattered throughout the country...like the Pennsylvania Dutch. If they won't use cars, there's no way they owned DOTS. Same with tribes in Amazonia. Religious cults in the desert Southwest. The poor who couldn't afford upgrading to 7G. And, of course, some people like you and me who just had the fortune — or misfortune, perhaps–of having them out at the time."

His words infused Alyssa with new hope. There was still a chance her mom was alive. That for some reason she'd taken her DOTS out that night. And Tucker. He'd still be waiting for her. She had to go back for him.

"Yeah, I'm sure there's lots of people who made it," Erik continued, his voice turning grim. "But I'm not worried about them."

Alyssa spun her head to study him. Even in the warmth of the sun, his rosy face turned suddenly pallid.

"It won't take long for others to find out." Erik's brows knit with worry. "And to be honest, I don't want to be here when they arrive."

Studying him for a moment, Alyssa contemplated his implications. Looters ransacking the stores. Terrorists hiding out in the Caribbean. Detainees from the reopened Guantánamo Bay. Maybe worse.

"But if we drive north?" Alyssa suggested, optimistic once more. Then she could stop by her home on the way. She had to see her mother one last time–just to know for sure.

"I already thought about that. Canada's gotta be gone. They leapt onto the Conversion at the last minute. Who knows how many other countries did, too. To be honest, I don't think there's anywhere safe. Not anymore."

"So what's wrong with staying?" If the Pennsylvania Dutch didn't even know about the apocalyptic conversion, maybe she and Erik could find a safe haven with them.

"Think Wild West times ten."

Why did he have to be so vague? Yet in the pit of her stomach she knew he was right. Surveillance teams would come to scout out the area. Then others dressed in biohazard suits would arrive to clear the city, the country. She imagined flames from funeral pyres reaching high into the sky. But the cleanup or threat of disease wasn't Alyssa's biggest concern. It was what came next.

Invasion. Most likely by terrorist organizations, Alyssa assumed. An entire country laid free at their disposal. Anarchy would reign for a period of time, until some dictator stepped in to assume control. And to move from chaos to control could only happen if he ruled with an iron fist. She hoped the others could get out in time, before their lives were condemned to slavery. Or worse.

Subconsciously, Alyssa rubbed her neck, as if the dictatorial fist wrapped its fingers securely around her throat. She thought of the limited freedom awarded women in the Middle East–one of the reasons her father was sent there in the first place. But chances were she wouldn't even survive to see that day. Their only hope was to flee before the others arrived.

"Listen. I need you," Erik pleaded, breaking the silence. "I can't get out of here alone."

"But I promised." She reached inside her pocket, fingering Justin Hidalgo's dolphin pin. There would be no funeral for him. Not for any of them. His family deserved to know the truth. To own one memento of their deceased son. And she couldn't even accomplish that. Not if what Erik claimed was true.

Defeated, she buried her face in her hands. After a few minutes of sustained silence, she composed herself enough to murmur, "Okay. So what's your plan?"

Chapter Thirty-Seven

"You're out of your mind. I'm not doing it," Alyssa grumbled, blowing the unkempt hair from her face.

"It's not so bad. All you have to do is dump out the body—"

"No way," she retorted. "You don't know what I've been through."

"I've been through a lot, too. But it's the only way."

"I can't." Alyssa crossed her arms over her chest, refusing to meet his gaze.

Erik laid a gentle hand on her shoulder. "Why not?" he pressed.

She shrugged off his hand. "I just can't...o-kay!"

Erik sighed, frustrated. She was nothing like Rachael. Naturally, Rachael would be upset in this situation, too–who wouldn't't've?—but she was tougher than she looked. Rachael would've stepped up to her responsibilities. Accept fate as it was dealt her.

And to think Erik had experienced momentary relief when he happened across a survivor. And not just any survivor, but a sailor. Almost like Rachael was up there looking out for him, whispering her request in the ear of an angel.

Besides, if Erik could do this himself, then he would. But the Goldman's boat was too large for him to maneuver alone. He didn't dare take someone's he didn't know. Convincing himself that he only borrowed their boat was much easier to stomach than deliberately stealing a stranger's property. He certainly didn't need another guilt trip weighing on his soul. It was bad enough losing Rachael without giving her the chance to explain. To abandon anyone here would be nothing short of inhumane.

He reached inside the open window of a nearby car. Ignoring the stench of the bodies left inside, he pulled a pen and notepad from the glove box. Thinking hard, he scribbled out a list and thrust the paper at Alyssa.

"Okay. Fine. I'll get a car and you check out those shops over there." He pointed down the street. Across from the hotels stood one trinket shop after another. "We'll meet back at the boat."

Alyssa rubbed her tired eyes with her knuckles and nodded indifferently. Glancing at the list, she headed down the street in search of supplies.

Erik watched her depart, wondering if he'd made a huge mistake. He fingered his nose. It was tender all right, but he doubted she broke it. And the bleeding had ceased, though he wouldn't be surprised if his eyes turned black-and-blue. He had a deep bruise on his shinbone. Plus, she'd really nailed him where it counted.

But she was strong, he admitted, if only he could funnel that anger toward helping his cause. The whole thing was a simple misunderstanding, right?

Then why was he wary of trusting her?

So far she hadn't tried to run away again. Besides, where would she go? She'd figure out soon enough that he was her only chance for escape. But maybe he should've insisted they stay together–especially when he knew her search would be hopeless. She'd never find anything they needed, not in this touristy part of town. But at least she'd be close to the harbor.

He waited until she entered the first store, then turned in the opposite direction down the road. Erik checked four parked trucks before he found one with the keys still in the ignition. Crinkling his nose, he slid the driver's inert body out the door, dragging it away from the car so he wouldn't run it over on his way out. He wasn't sure he could handle the sound of tires crushing a corpse. (It was bad enough having to touch a steering wheel caked with dried blood.)

Closing his eyes momentarily, Erik turned the key and held his breath as the engine revved to life. Thank God, he thought as he shifted into reverse, it's got half a tank left. Pulling out of the parallel parking space, he ran through his mental list of which stores to hit while trying to ignore the devastation surrounding him.

Erik knew he had to escape Miami before he lost his mind. One can only disregard this much death for so long before it whittled away at your soul. Well, at least he found Alyssa. Even if fragile and emotionally scarred, she was better than nothing.

Regardless, he couldn't leave her here by herself. Not in good conscience. Not with who would undoubtedly arrive soon. Erik shuddered at the thought.

He hoped she'd find everything on the list. He hoped she'd return to the boat before him. And above all, he hoped they could make it out of the harbor in time.

Chapter Thirty-Eight

Dump out the body. How sick and malicious could he be? Of all the people to find left alive, she had to run into a callous, coldhearted excuse for a soul. Figures. And now he expected her to sail off into the unknown with him.

Like that would ever happen.

Alyssa ambled down the sidewalk, conscious of the fact that he eyed her with suspicion. She purposefully held the paper at arms-reach to make out his hurried scrawl. It read:

Golden Sunset, Slip 32

What a cheesy name for a boat, she thought, rolling her eyes. Her eyes scanned the rest of his list:

food
water
clothes
first aid kit
binoculars
towels
sunscreen
swimsuits

Typical stuff you'd need to survive an emergency.

But she had no intention of finding the items he requested. She only hoped he didn't know that...yet.

Alyssa stuffed the list into her pocket and swallowed hard as she stared down the street. A chill running down her spine, she dared another peek over her shoulder. Was he still watching her? Yep. So for now, she must give the impression of sticking to his plan.

The sidewalk was littered with bodies: couples and families collapsed upon one another, toddlers slumped sideways in strollers, shopping bags strewn across the ground, their contents scattered. And everywhere, the flies. Buzzing around the dried blood crusted over the eyes and ears of the fallen. Even the sea breeze couldn't blow away the odor that lingered in the midday heat.

Alyssa's eyes burned. She plugged her nose. This wasn't right. She shouldn't be here. She should've died like her crew, hundreds of feet beneath the sea. Not stuck here in a nightmare of apocalyptic proportions.

Suddenly, she knew what she had to do. Suppressing the rising feelings of guilt at abandoning the sole survivor she'd encountered thus far, she darted inside the first shop on the street. Overhead, a red flag with a diagonal white stripe painted onto a wooden sign creaked in the breeze.

At least the characteristic smell of wetsuit neoprene countered the reek of the few individuals left inside. Empty scuba tanks lined the walls while glass-fronted cases displayed expensive sets of masks and snorkel gear. Alyssa had only stepped inside to escape Erik's watchful glare. There wasn't anything in here she would need. Nevertheless, she couldn't afford to arouse his suspicions further; not after he'd caught up to her so quickly before. So she meandered through racks of rash guards, short and full-length wetsuits, and T-shirts with lewd depictions of various versions of "diving" until she reached the cashier counter in the back of the store. Stepping over a customer sprawled across the floor, Alyssa peeked over the counter. In the middle of a transaction, the employee had left the cash register wide open, untouched.

Gingerly, Alyssa walked around the counter, twisting to avoid stepping on the dead cashier. She nervously glanced over her shoulder, half expecting to spot Erik at the front door. Before letting herself second-guess her actions, she filled a plastic shopping bag with the contents of the cash register. This should be more than enough for now, she thought.

Then she lifted up the empty drawer of bills to peer underneath, finding a lighter, a set of car keys, and a Smith and Wesson 9 millimeter semi-automatic. Her finger grazed the black barrel. Combat simulation was one thing; this was real life. It wasn't really her style…and yet.

Biting her lip, Alyssa drummed her fingers across the counter, deliberating her next course of action. She picked up the set of keys and aimed them out the back window. Pressing the lock button, she heard a friendly beep, beep from behind the store. Alyssa smiled in smug satisfaction.

Erik will be waiting back at the boat, she reminded herself. But when she reached inside her pocket to take a second look at his list, her fingers grazed Justin Hidalgo's dolphin pin. Alyssa's heart leapt up her throat. With fresh determination, she stuffed the lighter and keys into her pocket, grabbed the gun and bag of bills, and marched out the back door.

Chapter Thirty-Nine

Erik spent the better part of the morning gathering supplies. At least that's what he convinced himself he was doing. Did it count as stealing and grand theft auto if no one was around to witness his acts?

Taking side streets and driving over the sidewalks, he successfully dodged most of the congestion of stalled cars (and he'd thought Miami's traffic was horrendous before!), finally making it out of downtown. He hit half a dozen stores, each time blocking out the stench of decay that filled his nostrils while he stuffed bag after bag with non-perishable food items, clothes, charcoal, and water. Lots of bottled water.

Erik loaded the goods into the tailgate, then began the laborious process of winding his way through one jam after another to return to the harbor. He hoped he hadn't kept Alyssa waiting too long. Would she even wait? Erik wondered, or sail off without me? It was a moot question. Either the boat was there or it wasn't. There was nothing he could do about that now.

Pulling into the harbor, Erik stopped the car at the end of the dock in the NO PARKING ZONE. Grabbing armfuls of goods from the tailgate, he hauled the supplies down the dock, relieved to see the Goldmans' slip still occupied. Phew, he thought. She hadn't left without him after all.

With a groan, Erik heaved the bags onto the boat. "Did you find everything, Alyssa?" he called as he climbed onboard.

He paused, waiting for a response. But the only sound he heard was the water rocking against the hull of the ship. In an instant, his stomach filled with dread.

Running down the steps to the cabin, he dumped the bags on the floor, then checked the bedroom. Empty, Erik frowned. He knocked on the door to the head. "Alyssa?" he called again, louder this time. Still no answer. Taking a deep breath, he opened the door. Empty as well.

Where could she be?

Erik bolted back up the stairs, squinted into the bright sunlight shimmering across the surface of the harbor. He brushed his blonde bangs from his eyes as he scanned the dock for some sign of activity. Aside from the swaying masts and rustling palm fronds, he saw nothing.

So what's keeping her? She should be back by now. He pounded his fist on the gunwale, scolding himself for agreeing to split up. Worse, Erik had no way of contacting her; all he could do was wait. "How did people ever survive before cell phones?" he groaned as he returned to the truck for another load of supplies.

With each trip to the boat, the pit in Erik's stomach deepened. By the time he finished stowing the last of the items haphazardly in the cabin, she miraculously returned. But Erik's jaw hit the floor as he noticed only a small shopping bag slung over her shoulder. What was she thinking?!

"What took you so long?" Erik barked as he leapt over the side of the boat. With unspoken frustration, his arms tensed at his sides, his hands balling into fists.

Alyssa didn't answer as she stared off into the distance, her face drained of color. She staggered down the dock, one sluggish step after another.

Erik snatched the bag from over her shoulder. He rummaged through, finding only a heap of bills. "What about food? The binoculars?" he complained. "The medical kit? And the sunscreen?"

Speechless, Alyssa blinked, meeting his glare with steely hazel eyes.

What had she been doing this whole time? Erik released a heavy sigh. Of all the people he had to find alive, why couldn't he at least have gotten someone helpful? Even squeamish Rachael who fainted at the sight of her own blood would've done better. Maybe he was right: he'd made a huge mistake asking her to come.

Not that it mattered now. It wouldn't be long before someone else arrived. To be honest, he'd rather not stick around and wait for that to happen. Making a small attempt at consoling her, Erik helped her step on board.

"So…are you all set to go?"

She plopped down onto the bench without a word.

Erik's blood began to boil. "Can you give me a hand with these lines?"

She turned her head, refusing to meet his gaze.

"Seriously," he continued, straining to keep a civil tone. "I don't think I can push off myself."

Silently, Alyssa rose off the bench.

Thank God, thought Erik as he tossed her one end of the nylon rope. Instead, she looked at him in a baffled way, letting the rope fall to her feet. Then she slunk down the stairs, winding her way through the piles of bags to lie on the sole double bed in the cabin. Dumbfounded, Erik peered below, finding her curled up in a ball. Her eyes appeared blank and distant, almost catatonic.

"Thanks for your help," Erik called, heavy on the sarcasm. "I'll take it from here, I guess." He tromped across the deck, preparing to cast off.

What had he gotten himself into? Rachael had no leverage up there, did she? Or maybe this was her way of getting back at him after all.

Frowning miserably, Erik snuck a peek at the horizon again. The sun dipped low in the sky, casting a reddish glow over the water. At least the sea looked clear…so far. He had no doubt they'd make it out of the harbor in time. He only hoped he'd be able to put a safe distance between them and any approaching ships before nightfall.

Chapter Forty

The first night passed without a hitch. Well, not exactly. But at least Erik didn't capsize the Goldmans' boat.

Erik spent the first few hours cursing himself for not taking his parents up on that offer to go sailing earlier this semester. He really needed someone to jog his memory in how to tack and jibe, but that person refused to leave the cabin.

On more than one occasion Erik lost the evening wind, only to gain it back in full force suddenly, whipping the boom around…and almost whacking him in the head. Finally, with the sun deep below the horizon and the stars as bright pinpricks in the black velvet above, he settled on safely sailing with the jib alone.

It wasn't like he could sleep anyway, not with the ghastly images of his loved ones' bodies filling his mind. So for hours Erik sat there, listening with his good ear to the lopsided breeze rippling the jib sheet and Alyssa intermittently dashing to the head, wondering how he got himself into this mess.

Some sailor Alyssa turned out to be. He lost count of the number of times she got seasick that first night. Afraid of the vile smell churning his stomach as well, Erik only ventured into the cabin when pushing liquids on her to prevent dehydration. But she never kept them down for long.

It wasn't like the seas were that rocky, either. How she ever managed aboard a Navy ship was beyond him. Erik should've thought of putting seasickness patches on her list back in Miami. Then he remembered that wouldn't't've helped.

Not when she disregarded everything he bothered to write.

Not until the middle of the next day, with Miami far in the distance, did Alyssa finally emerge from the cabin, tying her washed uniform to a handhold to dry. She'd made an effort to shower and put on a fresh, white buttoned-down shirt and a pair of khaki shorts the Goldmans must've left below, but her face still wore a sickly color of puce.

Keeping his hand on the tiller, Erik studied her warily. "Feeling better?" he asked, more to hear his own voice than expecting an answer.

With shaking hands, she grasped one handhold after another, finally settling silently onto the bench in the cockpit.

Solitude was infinitely better than being ignored, Erik decided. He cranked the winch to take in the sails and prepare to come about.

In the midst of his activity, Erik thought he heard her speak. He let up on the winch, turning his left ear toward the helpless lump on the bench named Alyssa.

"Did you say something?"

Alyssa wiped her brow, then wrapped her arms around her waist, shivering slightly. "I'm sorry," she repeated softly, hesitantly glancing at Erik.

Erik blinked. Relying solely on his hazy knowledge of sailing, he'd pushed the Golden Sunset off and unfurled the sails without her. She'd been nothing but a hassle so far. And now she was apologizing. It didn't make up for her lack of effort, but it was a start.

"I'm sorry I made you wait so long," She continued, her shoulders slumping forward. "I didn't believe you at first. So I left. I had to see for myself."

Erik's face fell. So that's what took her so long–she hadn't planned to come back at all. Well, maybe it would've been better if she hadn't returned. Maybe he'd prefer solitude's slow trip to insanity, rather than his unsuccessful attempts at reading her thoughts.

Alyssa looked away again, probably hurt by his expression. "But when I got out of town, I realized you were right." Her voice faltered, slightly hoarse. "It was everywhere, not just on the sub. I couldn't get past the stalled cars. All the roads–blocked. With death."

Erik nodded, his hands frozen on the winch, waiting for her to continue. The jib sail flapped unhappily in the breeze, but he paid it no attention.

"You were right," her voice trembled, melancholy in tone. "There wasn't anything left to go back to."

Then she did that fading-out thing again: the blank stare into the distance. Erik wondered what thoughts passed through her head as he set back to work trimming the jib sail. Could he even count on her for assistance in the future?

"I promised my mother I'd return," Alyssa eventually continued, more to herself than to him. "I never said goodbye. Not to my mom. My friends. No one." She shivered again, hugging herself tighter.

Erik's hand let up on the rope as he dropped his head, overcome with guilt. Maybe he'd been too hard on her this whole time. It wasn't easy for him, either. Not in the least. He'd wanted to give up, too…until he remembered Rachael.

He could still hear her voice, coaxing him to press forward. Somehow, to find a way to survive.

Erik crossed the cockpit to lock off the tiller. Then he sat down on the opposite bench. Managing a sympathetic smile, he said, "It's not your fault. I know how you feel. My parents. And my sister. I saw them." His body shuddered at the recollection. "Can you believe I was going to be an uncle? She hadn't told us yet."

But she'd tried, he reminded himself. If I'd been smart enough to see the signs. "Well, not directly."

He didn't know why he felt compelled to share Kristen's news with her. Maybe he simply needed to tell someone. Just to get it off his chest, perhaps.

While Erik bent his head to wipe his eyes on his sleeve, he jostled the tiller slightly. The rudder turned the boat to starboard, making the sail flop restlessly. He let it stay that way. Might as well get the rest out...while she was listening. He felt better telling someone, even if that someone was reluctant to respond.

"It's not just that," Erik continued, feeling the weight gradually lift from his soul. "My girlfriend, too." The image of Rachael hugging Jamie outside of class rushed into his mind. Erik gnashed his teeth. "If I hadn't been so pissed at her, I wouldn't be here right now."

"You can't blame yourself for that," Alyssa said sympathetically. Sliding down the bench, she reached across the cockpit to place her hand gently upon his knee.

Erik stiffened briefly. Was she slipping out of her trance, becoming human once more? So why did he react in such a frightened way? This was what he wanted: companionship, camaraderie, someone to share the burden he bore. Wasn't it?

It took Erik a minute to remember where he was going with his thoughts. If he stopped his confession now, he'd risk losing her all over again.

As difficult as it was to recall the horrendous memories, he persisted, "No. It's true." A single tear slid down his cheek. His voice choked on the words, "I thought she was cheating on me. Turns out it was her cousin, up visiting for the weekend. She was just showing him around campus."

He leaned forward, his head falling into his palms. His shoulders heaved with silent sorrow. Managing a forced chuckle, he added, "I only took my DOTS out 'cause I couldn't stand her constant messages. Go figure she was just trying to explain."

Alyssa's hand left his knee. Surprisingly, she got up to sit next to him, softly patting his back in consolation.

Erik shook his head sadly. He lifted his eyes to gaze across the horizon containing nothing but the wide blue sea. What was the point in continuing? It didn't matter that Alyssa was finally opening up to him. He'd lost the love of his life. Nothing could change that. And he'd be with Rachael now–in a better place than this ruined world–if only he'd listened...

All of a sudden, everything seemed remarkably insignificant. The warmth of Alyssa's hand on his back faded. Even the beating sun failed to reach his core.

"But y'know what? Sometimes I wish I had listened," he admitted in a weak voice. "Sometimes I wish I wasn't here anymore."

Quietly, Alyssa removed her arm from his shoulders and slogged out of the cockpit. Nice one, Erik. You screwed things up again. Why had he bothered opening up to her? It'd done nothing but augment his misery.

Alyssa' footsteps dropped like lead weights upon the stairs as she headed down into the cabin, leaving Erik alone to ponder his uncertain future. And whether he would've been better off by himself.

Chapter Forty-One

Hours later, Alyssa dragged herself off the bed in the cabin. As much as she desired space from Erik and his reminders of those she'd lost, she gagged on the stuffy air below, filled with the reek of illness. Even sliding open the small windows to allow the breeze to pass through offered little reprieve from the overwhelming sadness clogging her throat. Suddenly the stale, dark air of the Siren buzzing with active submariners didn't seem so lousy after all.

Like it or not, this was her fate: doomed to a small boat with the only living person she'd encountered. Face it, Alyssa, she scolded herself, anyone left alive would remind you of Justin or Mom. Instinctively, she felt for Justin's dolphin pin in the pocket of her borrowed shorts. Seeking comfort, she carried it with her always.

Maybe things with Erik would improve if she tried speaking to him again. Then again, maybe it wouldn't. But at least she could let go of some of the burden heaped upon her weary shoulders. Besides, she could only avoid him for so long in this limited space.

Trudging up the stairs, she deposited herself on the side of the boat, hugging her knees as she stared at the whitecaps beyond.

For several minutes, she sensed Erik's eyes bearing upon her, as if waiting for her to speak. The problem was she didn't know where to begin.

Luckily, she didn't have to. All of a sudden, the sail fell limp. She heard Erik's footsteps cross the cockpit. Glancing over her shoulder, she met his gaze with saddened eyes.

"Listen," Erik said, his face softening, "I'm sorry. I shouldn't have been so hard on you. I just assumed since you were in the Navy, you could help out with the sailing." Then he bit his lip, like he should've stopped when he was ahead.

She let it slide. He was right to feel hurt—she'd been useless thus far. Not until she got stuck in Miami's traffic, unable to make it out of town, did Alyssa realize Erik might be her only hope. But since she'd returned, he'd been so judgmental, making the hairs on the back of her neck bristle every time he spoke. He didn't know anything about her, or what she'd been through.

Then maybe you should tell him, she reminded herself. After all, he'd already confided in her. Weren't they supposed to work together as a team to get to wherever they were headed? Though deep down, she doubted Erik knew their final destination, either.

"I am in the Navy," Alyssa began before she lost her nerve. "Make that, was, I s'pose, given the state of things." She heaved a deep sigh. "But I didn't sail on a ship. I was assigned to a sub. Conducting sonar tests in the Caribbean and the Atlantic." Instantly, Alyssa regretted her last statement. Was that information still classified if the U.S. military was nonexistent?

Erik's eyebrows knitted together. He probably didn't realize the dolphin insignia on her uniform was exclusive to the submariner force. Most civilians would've drawn a similar conclusion.

"Then how did you end up here? In Miami, I mean?" he ventured.

So Alyssa related her story (purposefully omitting her romantic interlude with Officer Justin Hidalgo, of course) from training at Sub School to the sonar tests to the whale fatalities to breaking her stint in Quarantine. As she spoke, she noticed Erik's attitude gradually change. It was slight at first, bordering on disbelief. (Though how could anyone contrive such a harrowing tale?)

But when she reached the part about finding the entire crew perished and the sub sinking, with her only escape lying in successful use of the egress chamber, Erik's initial disbelief transformed into an expression of profound awe. His jaw crept toward the floor as he regarded her anew, instantly excusing the initial panic in her desperate need to locate a search and rescue team to recover the submarine. Or her reluctance to obtain a vehicle to scour Miami's shops for provisions.

Emotionally depleted, Alyssa concluded with the red Porsche bearing down on her—the Porsche he was driving. Cautiously, she glanced at Erik, gauging his reaction. He simply stared back at her, speechless.

In the awkward silence that followed, the light chop of the sea seemed amplified, echoing against the hull of the ship. She shuddered as the chilling ocean spray kicked over the side of the boat, reminding her of how close she was to death only a short while ago.

Alyssa dropped onto the cockpit bench, rubbing her hands up and down her arms. She had expected to feel some relief from sharing this news. Instead, the cavity within her chest widened, as if her heart had sunk into the abysmal depths with the Siren and its crew. She felt a sudden pang of longing for the familiarity of the life she had previously been so eager to escape.

What was she thinking; reliving the horrific memories of seeing her friends and the guy she loved slumped over in pools of their own blood? How could recounting it a million times ever make it hurt less?

"I feel so callous," Alyssa continued weakly. Her eyes fell to her feet. "Like a monster. I don't have any tears left."

"You're not a monster," Erik said softly as he sat down next to her. Their unbalanced weight tilted the boat slightly to port. Neither appeared to mind.

Placing his index finger on the base of her jaw, Erik raised her head to meet his gaze. Her eyes locked with his for a lasting moment.

"I know it sounds pretty ridiculous now," he added with a small, sheepish grin, "but when I saw your uniform, I assumed you were stationed at the base in Miami. Or on one of the boats in the harbor. I never imagined you were trapped..." he shivered slightly, "underwater."

Gently, his fingertips brushed her cheekbone as he smoothed her windswept hair from her face. His hand glazed across the back of her head, his palm finally resting against the nape of her neck. Alyssa felt her head melt into his hand with the reassurance of his warm touch.

As her eyes searched his, everything made sense. His insensible reluctance to allow her to find help. His insufferable demands to find supplies. And his incomprehensible anger when she returned empty-handed.

All this time, he had no idea of the agony she had endured.

Alyssa opened her mouth to speak. But before she could verbalize a response to excuse Erik's past behavior, his lips suddenly found hers. Softly, tenderly, he kissed her, as if apologizing for the misunderstanding that forged the basis of their relationship. His fingers passed across her knotted shoulders on their way down her spine, pausing momentarily at her waist to draw her body toward his. Alyssa breathed deeply as his lips left hers to trace the length of her jawbone, then caress the base of her throat.

Alyssa closed her eyes, consumed with a calming sensation of safety, comfort, and earned respect. Thrown into each other's lives by extenuating circumstances, they now found themselves dependent upon each other. The indifferent stranger before her had vanished. Erik had become her confidant. Her partner in their struggle for survival.

And the only soul she knew alive in this uncertain world.

Slowly, Alyssa wound her arms around his back, her lips anxious for his soothing touch, ready to join his once more. Though this kiss lacked the reckless passion of her clandestine encounter with Officer Hidalgo in the Mess Hall, it was far sweeter. Deeper. And more meaningful, like two souls united in mutual grief.

For the first time since her nearly fatal ascent to the surface, Alyssa felt invigorated, her anxieties erased, her nerves steeled once more. Opening her eyes, she broke away to smile up at him, lightly running her fingers through his waves of blonde hair. Erik returned her smile, obviously pleased — perhaps even relieved-by the unexpected turn of events.

As Alyssa leaned forward to resume their kiss, something near the horizon caught her attention. She squinted into the blanket of night, spotting a flickering light against the darkened sea.

"Oh, God," she moaned through trembling lips. "We've got company."

Erik's hands froze on her waist. His face paled in the thin light of the waning moon.

Quickly, Alyssa ducked out of his embrace and leapt down the stairs to extinguish the cabin lights, certain this sign could be either quite promising...or utterly disastrous.

Chapter Forty-Two

"Alyssa?" Erik called down from the cockpit as he unfurled the mainsail, "What're you doing?"

"Getting ready," she grunted under the strain of lifting a heavy crate.

He'd heard Alyssa for quite some time, rummaging through the piles of supplies in the darkened cabin while muttering curses under her breath. Erik wondered what had sparked her sudden interest.

Keeping the tiller aimed as far west of the approaching light as possible, Erik squinted into the dim moonlight, studying Alyssa quizzically as she collected items–for what purpose, he could not fathom.

Then Alyssa yelped as a stack of boxes crashed upon her.

Erik winced. "You okay down there?"

"Peachy," came her muffled reply.

Well, at least she'd begun pulling her own weight. Rescuing her had been the noble course of action. Perhaps he was a little hasty in kissing her, he admitted, though Alyssa didn't seem to mind. Besides, Rachael would understand. She was gone, so she'd want him to find comfort in her loss, wouldn't she? It was only the beginning of the long and arduous process to mend his shattered heart.

Nervously, Erik glanced over his shoulder again. The flickering light had indeed gotten closer. But when he squinted into the blackness beyond, he could not discern an island's silhouette behind it. Which could only mean one thing.

It belonged to another boat.

Under different circumstances, Erik would have been thrilled at the prospect of encountering other survivors. Logically, pockets of civilization remained. The poor in third world countries who couldn't afford the technology, though commonplace in the U.S. and other developed nations. Remote groups of extremists scattered throughout the country. Some terrorists, most likely. And pirates.

A valid reason to worry. Why wait to find out the other sailors' intentions?

She soon returned topside, her arms loaded with a couple of T-shirts and bottles of vodka, rum, and whiskey that Erik had pilfered from a liquor store in Miami.

Erik raised his eyebrows. "What's that for?"

"A surprise for our guests." Her forehead beaded with perspiration as she pushed her short, tangled brown hair behind her ears, adding, "Just in case."

Erik found her elusiveness irritating. She wasn't at all like Rachael, who spoke her mind and then some. But maybe that's okay. If Erik had bothered to stop for a minute and listen to Rachael–instead of spinning a web of accusations and lies–he'd be dead, too.

Grumbling to himself, Erik tried to imagine what Alyssa planned to do with half his stash of alcohol on board. He might need it later to drown his sorrows. Once he could pause for a moment and properly mourn the loss of everyone he knew. And loved.

And yet, in a quirky way, Erik found Alyssa's concentration and determination somewhat alluring, as if her brain had instantly shifted into high alert, entering a sort of survival mode. Combined with her courageous tale of escaping, maybe there was more to Alyssa than he imagined. Part of him decided he'd like to find out.

Erik watched her with growing interest as she struggled to tear long strips from the lame FLORIDA BEACH BUM tees he'd snatched off a rack at the grocery store. Not like he planned to wear them or anything, he merely thought the fabric might come in handy. Plus they were the only things he could find in his haste to return to the Goldmans' boat.

"Need some help?" he offered.

She shook her head. "Nah. I'm good."

Wistfully, he watched her work, tearing the shirts into strips and stuffing one end into each of the bottles of alcohol sadly going to waste. Her brow furrowed with concentration as her eyes repeatedly darted to the sea, monitoring their progress.

Finished with her task, she set the bottles neatly in a row, tapping her pockets until she pulled out a lighter. She knelt down to test the lighter, shielding its warm glow from the wind and sight of the other ship. Satisfied, she stuffed it back inside her pocket, pacing as she contemplated her next course of action.

"Think they're friendly?" she wondered, her agitated eyes scanning the horizon.

"I dunno. But I don't really want to stick around to find out." Erik adjusted the sails and rigging, trying to build speed.

She flicked her eyes toward the engine sitting idle. "Should we start her up?"

"Maybe. Or do you think it might give them more of a reason to pursue us? If they thought we were running away?"

"Good point." She peered again at the growing light. "They're still gaining on us."

Erik didn't reply. He was thinking about how much he'd like a pair of binoculars to get a closer look at the approaching boat and the numbers aboard. Yet he'd already chewed Alyssa out enough for her lack of help back in Miami.

At the time, he hadn't known the extent of the trials she'd endured. And now–despite everything she'd been through — she was ready to fight for their lives.

Chapter Forty-Three

"GET DOWN!" Alyssa ordered. She pushed Erik flat on his belly just as a bullet whizzed past their heads, puncturing the mainsail. Prone against the floor of the cockpit, Alyssa turned her head toward Erik. "Still think they're friendly?" she said sardonically as another shot screamed over the gunwale.

Too afraid to speak, Erik hoped her question was rhetorical. Here they were–being shot at–and she was cracking jokes. What a warped sense of humor.

After a third bullet sailed overhead, Alyssa got up from their hiding spot and leaped down the stairs into the cabin. Where's she going now? Erik wondered; petrified to move a finger, much less leave his spot on the floor. Within seconds she returned carrying a small handgun.

"Where'd you get that?" Erik gasped, his face drained of color.

Alyssa shrugged. "Something I picked up when shopping in town." She nestled herself against the gunwale, squinting her left eye to aim at the approaching boat.

Erik lifted his head enough to watch her first shot. His stomach fluttered uneasily. Who is this person? Certainly not the same incompetent wreck he'd pulled off the street. He managed to squeak out a few words, "But how'd you know how to—?"

"What?" she asked, dodging below the gunwale for a moment as the other boat returned fire. "Shoot a gun? From weapons and defense tactics training, I guess. Kind of a required thing." She scampered back to her knees, took aim, and fired again.

How can she be so nonchalant? Erik shuddered as he heard a loud splash in the distance. She just killed a man.

Erik had never gone hunting, never even held a real gun before. The closest he came was playing paintball with some guys in college a couple of times. Eventually, however, he lost interest–due largely in part to the series of circular welts across his back when his roommate, Lucas Jenkins, tagged him at close range in enemy territory.

He swallowed hard thinking about Lucas and the guys, and the mock reality of their game. Only this was no game. Here, his life was at stake. And he felt utterly helpless in protecting it.

Alyssa, on the other hand, appeared completely in her element, as if conducting a mere training exercise. She seemed cool and collected, while Erik couldn't stop the sweat from pouring down his brow. Secretly, he thanked Rachael. What would he have done in this situation, alone?

Erik watched Alyssa aim and pick off three more men in succession, his jaw dropping to the floor. Not just any men, but pirates, no doubt. Just thinking about the word made his skin crawl. He'd always thought of pirates as historic fiction from the early days of Caribbean settlements. He never expected to actually endure an attack by pirates. And if captured, these men certainly wouldn't bother to hold them for ransom…not after 7G. So that meant only one thing.

The men aboard that ship would stop at nothing to kill them both and take claim of the Golden Sunset and all their supplies onboard. A shiver of fear racked Erik's spine.

Alyssa shot again. Erik heard a splash as a body fell overboard. Then the firing ceased.

"Think you got him."

"Yep," Alyssa nodded. "But it's not over yet." Spotting two men still standing, she set aim and clicked the trigger. Only this time, nothing happened. She popped open the magazine, finding no rounds remaining.

"Well," she said grimly, "I guess we wait."

"How many do you think are left?" Erik ventured. His voice cracked mid-sentence.

Alyssa shrugged. "I counted two."

That's good, Erik thought. One for each of us.

"But who knows how many are waiting below."

Erik's stomach flipped upside down. Each passing minute seemed like an hour as he huddled next to Alyssa in the cockpit, sneaking peeks at the approaching ship. His body shook with anticipation. Would he be able to kill someone in defense, like Alyssa had so easily done? Would he risk losing her because he was too afraid to fight?

A vice gripped Erik's heart, crushing it once more. He'd already lost Rachael without confessing his true feelings. If he was about to meet his end, he didn't want to take that chance again. His eyes glistened over, fearing the worst. In desperation, his fingers sought Alyssa's, squeezing them tightly. Alyssa met his worried gaze.

"If anything should happen," he began, "I want you to know that—"

She smiled confidently. "Don't worry. Nothing will happen."

"It's just that…" Erik frowned as the words got stuck in his throat.

"Nothing." She returned his squeeze. "I promise."

He tried to smile back, but it came out as a strained grimace. Alyssa didn't seem to notice. She released his hand, her attention once again focused on the approaching ship. With his good ear, Erik detected the splashing of water against the hull of the other boat and the purr of the engine's motor, closing the gap. Quickly, Alyssa reached for one of her bottles, flicking the lighter to ignite the scrap of shirt fabric sticking out the end.

Erik finally understood. She'd assembled a series of firebombs.

Rising to her knees, she launched the flaming bottle over the side of the boat. Erik watched the tongues of fire lap the dark night as the bomb sailed over the water, landing helplessly in the deep, black sea. Alyssa swore under her breath as she lit a second bottle and threw again. This time it splashed a few feet short of the ship, its flames instantly extinguished in the water's murky depths. With dismay, Erik glanced at the remaining bottles lined neatly in a row. Her supply rapidly dwindled.

When she reached for a third, Erik placed his hand on her wrist, stopping her. "Here. Let me," he offered. Grabbing the lighter from her, he flicked it until the T-shirt tail caught fire. Rising to his knees, he cocked his arm and released. The flaming bottle arced across the water, exploding on contact with the intruding boat. A series of panicked shouts in a language Erik didn't understand followed as the fire traveled up their mainsail halyard.

"Yes!" He exclaimed as he ducked back down, his fist pumping in jubilation. Pleased with himself, he grinned at Alyssa.

"How'd you do that?" She wore an exasperated look upon her face.

Erik shrugged. "I used to play third base."

She narrowed her eyes at him, but readily handed over the rest of the bottles. Adrenaline pumped like hot lava through his veins as Erik launched the last of her firebombs, successfully hitting the cockpit twice. Flames erupted around the boat; the pirates fought madly to extinguish the blazes. They cut the engine, but still approached steadily, flames and all, preparing to board the Golden Sunset.

Alyssa nudged Erik's arm. With a wink, she advised, "Get ready."

Erik's face turned green.

"It won't be so bad. Just try not to think about it too much." Smiling in an amused way, Alyssa leaned toward him, suddenly pressing her lips to his mouth. Time slowed to a crawl as her soft lips tenderly touched his. He closed his eyes, wishing to be anywhere but here, on the eve of this forthcoming battle. He yearned to hold her again, finding comfort in their closeness. To feel her heart beating against his chest in energetic bursts, unlike the multitude of silenced ones he'd encountered in the aftermath of 7G. To have her soothing fingers run through his hair, erasing the painful memories forever.

But time was cruel. Alyssa's lips left his as quickly as they met. She flew to her feet, just as the first pirate leapt across the water, successfully landing on the stern of the Sunset. Alyssa reached inside her pocket, pulling out a knife as she dashed across the cockpit to engage him.

Why didn't I think of that? Erik wondered as he warily rose, taking in his surroundings. Alyssa was right about one thing: there were more pirates concealed below. With dark faces covered in printed scarves, Erik couldn't determine their ethnicities. Possibly Middle Eastern or African in descent, he guessed. And he spotted five pirates remaining, making them easily outnumbered. A loud splash off the stern made Erik spin. Alyssa stood alone, waiting for the next to board.

Okay. Make that four remaining.

"A little help?" Alyssa shouted breathlessly as another pirate spanned the distance between their ships, closest to Erik.

Erik shook his head, clearing his thoughts. Get your game face on, he encouraged himself as he steadied his feet on the rocking boat while a pirate stepped toward him. Frantically, he searched for something to use to fight, but everything inside the cockpit was already attached.

Then he got an idea. While he heard Alyssa grunt and lunge at her attacker, Erik stepped backwards, inching toward the boom. The dark pirate readied his fist to swing at Erik. But Erik dropped the sail, placed both hands on the boom and shoved it at the man's face. Erik winced as he heard the metal crunch the man's skull, knocking him clear off the side of the boat.

Three left. He spun his head to see how Alyssa fared. She swung her blade at the pirate's chest, catching only air as the pirate backed away. But he didn't have time to assist as another man bore upon him. Erik turned toward the man, searching for a new plan when the pirate's knuckles met his face. Erik's head reeled as blood splattered from his nose. He fell backward into the cockpit, wiping his nostrils with the back of his hand.

Get up! he shouted at himself. You can't give up this easy! Erik balled his fists as he rose to his feet, swinging madly. Blood boiling, he threw a punch with his right fist, then his left. He hit the pirate in the gut and in the cheek, but it wasn't enough to stop the onslaught. The man hit Erik again, this time square in the belly. Erik doubled over in pain.

Your life. Alyssa's, too. The boat. He couldn't relent now. Gritting his teeth, Erik drew back his fist, aiming at the pirate's nose when he heard Alyssa yell.

"Wha—?" He wheeled his head around to hear with his good ear.

"DUCK!" she repeated, the hilt of a knife cocked behind her head...aimed directly at Erik's face. His eyes bulged. He'd seen her precision (or lack, thereof) with the firebombs before. Granted that was at a distance, but Erik wasn't ready to take the chance.

Erik immediately dropped to the floor of the cockpit. Laughing, the pirate stepped on Erik's ankle, crushing it beneath his boot, just as Alyssa aimed and released.

Erik roared in pain, hearing the bones in his ankle crunch under the weight of the boot. But the pressure soon relented. Erik glanced up, noticing the pirate's eyes growing dim...and Alyssa's blade lodged deep within the man's sternum. The pirate tumbled backwards, landing with a loud splash in the inky water. Two remaining, Erik counted.

Grasping a second knife in her hand, Alyssa spun around to confront another pirate. But she hesitated momentarily, switching the blade from her left hand to her right. In that wasted moment, the pirate kicked the blade from her hand, sending it scooting across the floor, out of reach.

"Watch out!" Erik screamed. Ignoring the burn in his ankle, he hopped to one foot, ramming his shoulder into the man's torso and sending him overboard into the deep. Then Erik collapsed onto the floor, his ankle searing with pain, unable to bear any more weight.

With utter dismay, he spotted the final pirate climbing up the side of their boat, his clothes dripping onto the deck as he reached for the knife Alyssa had dropped. Brandishing the blade, he inched toward Alyssa as a look of shock registered upon her face. In desperation, she searched her empty pockets, then balled her fists, ready for the fight.

Erik felt time slow to a crawl as he watched Alyssa fend off the attacker. He willed his body to protect her, to leap between her and the attacker, but he struggled to move, as if his feet were stuck in freshly poured concrete.

She ducked away from his jab to her chest; keeping her eyes trained on his every step. When he paused, Alyssa swung her fist, knocking him across the jaw. Blood sputtered from his mouth, splattering the inside of the cockpit. The pirate stepped backward, balancing precariously on the edge of the gunwale, like a cobra rearing its hooded head, waiting for the next opportunity to strike.

"It's over," the man hissed in a heavy accent as he lunged at Alyssa with the blade.

"Not a chance," Alyssa grinned wickedly, formulating a new plan in her head.

Erik watched Alyssa's hips twist sideways as her foot rose to meet the man's torso. The pirate slashed down hard with the knife in a last feeble attempt at defense. Alyssa raised her forearm to counter the blow as she kicked him hard in the gut. Grunting in pain, he tumbled over the side of the boat, gurgling as the inky water filled his open mouth and dragged him under.

But Alyssa lost her balance from the force of her blow. Erik gasped as he helplessly watched her topple backwards, whacking the back of her head on the metal boom. A resounding thud rocked Erik's heart as she collapsed, inert on the floor of the cockpit.

"NO!" Erik shouted as he crawled to her side, dragging his limp ankle behind. He bent over her, sweeping the hair from her face. "Alyssa!" he cried in desperation, clutching her hand in his.

Blood seeped from her wounded forearm, soaking her white sleeve a deep shade of crimson. For a moment, her eyes focused on his.

"You'll be alright," he smiled at her encouragingly. She had to be.

In a failing voice, Alyssa murmured, "I'm sorry, E-rik...I promised..."

Then her eyes grew dull. Her head fell listlessly to one side. Erik shook her gently, but her body had grown unresponsive.

"No, Alyssa. No," he begged, putting his head to her chest. What could he do now? And why hadn't he insisted they go back for a medical kit? Their rush to escape Miami suddenly seemed insignificant.

To think he might lose her now...just when he needed her most. Anguishing thoughts of a stark existence alone filled Erik's head as he cradled her passive body protectively, tears streaming down his cheeks.

Chapter Forty-Four

Alyssa fluttered her eyelids, squinting up at the scattered, wispy clouds glowing warm like sun-ripened peaches in the calm, early morning skies.

Blinking, she surveyed her surroundings. Her head ached brutally as she lay on the floor of the cockpit, despite the soft pillow placed beneath it. Erik had probably brought her here to monitor her condition while he sailed the ship. Blankets off the double bed covered her body, while her wounded arm carefully rested across the top. Even her blood-soaked sleeve had been cut away and her forearm freshly bandaged. Thank God Erik had been there to care for her.

Speaking of which, where was Erik? Maybe he'd gone below. Except he usually stayed near the tiller to keep the sails filled. Alyssa felt a pang of guilt for her lack of help since they set sail.

Then she paused, looking up. The sails. Perplexed, Alyssa stared at the folds of fabric lashed to the mast, the mainsail halyard rattling softly in the light breeze.

We've stopped. But why? Alyssa wondered.

Scowling in pain, she dragged herself up to peer over the starboard side. The anchor line was stretched taut. Confused, she slowly spun her head to look over the port gunwale.

The most remarkable sight greeted her...

All the photos Alyssa had accessed from the Siren's files during her stint underwater paled in comparison to the sight of impossible beauty lying before her now.

"Oh. My. God," Alyssa breathed, gazing upon the low, forested hills rolling into the sea, like a sapphire plunked in the middle of a huge basin of water dyed a brilliant turquoise. Spilling waves lapped at the white sandy beach. Tall palm trees filled with coconuts stretched far over the water. Nestled inside this protective cove, gentle waves bounced against the hull, lightly swaying the Sunset. The island was small–maybe a mile across at best. But after so long at sea, Alyssa couldn't help but think of the promise it held.

Suddenly she heard a rhythmic splashing on the side of the boat. A wave of relief passed over her as she kneeled to see Erik swimming toward the boat. His arms sliced through the water, dragging his limp leg behind. At the base of the ladder, he paused, grasping it tightly with his hands as he pulled himself one-legged to the top.

Before she could call his name, her eyes fell to Erik's tanned chest–stronger and leaner than when they'd departed Miami. His pectorals flexed as he hoisted himself over the side of the boat, dripping wet. Instantly, her tongue tied itself in a knot. Oh, my God, Alyssa thought, swallowing hard. Balancing on one leg, he shook the water from his ears. A frustrated look crossed his face as he tugged on his right earlobe — obviously still bothered by the loss of hearing on that side.

The tops of Erik's shoulders and cheeks were sunburned and starting to peel. Peeking at his foot, she realized why. He'd literally taken the shirt off his own back to wrap his foot, leaving the last remaining fresh cloth for her wounded arm. And she had neglected to bring a bottle of sunscreen like he'd asked, even though she probably could've found one at that scuba shop back in Miami.

Erik stepped gingerly onto the deck, wincing with pain. But his grimace quickly faded. His weary eyes flickered with joy at finding her conscious and awake.

"Hey! You're up! How're you feeling? I was afraid to leave you but..." The joyful look on his face vanished as he gritted his teeth to hobble across the deck.

Overlooking her own headache, Alyssa stood to meet him halfway, offering her hand as she helped him onto one of the cockpit's benches. It must've been hell for him to make all those trips down to the cabin while caring for her injuries.

"No worries. I just got up." Alyssa said, sitting across from him. "But, how did you..." Shamefaced, she paused. What were you gonna say...how'd you get here by yourself? Oh, please, Alyssa. It's not like you were much help even when you were conscious.

Instead, she settled for, "I mean...where are we?"

"Bahamas, I think, judging by the chart I found in the cabin." A wistful look filled his eyes.

Alyssa knew how he felt. With the DOTS, they would have known their precise location in a fraction of a second. But it's hard to miss something that robbed you of everything and everyone.

"So, have you checked out the place?" Alyssa asked, eager to distract her mind from the recurring thoughts of death.

He shook his head. "Can't do much with this bum ankle."

Alyssa frowned. "Sorry 'bout that."

"It's not your fault."

But Alyssa couldn't help but think that it was. Since she met him, she'd punched him in the schnoz, kicked him in the groin and the shin, and now rendered his ankle useless. If only she'd been faster throwing the knife. Or more accurate in launching the firebombs, she might've prevented the entire attack in the first place.

"The place looks deserted, though," Erik continued, easing the tension hanging in the air. "Might be a private island for a cruise ship or something." He handed her a pair of binoculars. "Here. Take a look."

Alyssa stared at the object in his hands, shocked. "Where'd you find those?"

"They were hidden in a drawer behind the cases of bottled water," Erik said, simpering with guilt for berating her back in Miami. Perhaps it hadn't mattered that she disregarded his entire list of supplies after all; the Golden Sunset came more stocked than she'd expected. But Alyssa couldn't hold him at blame for long. It served her right for all the pain she'd caused him.

Alyssa peered through the binoculars, focusing them as she scanned the beach. The island did have its possibilities: cabanas, rows of deck chairs stacked and locked in case of passing storms, and posts for a volleyball net. Well, they definitely had shelter–if they could break open the padlocks. Who knows? Maybe someone would even come back and find them here. Maybe.

"Nice spot," she grinned, passing Erik the binoculars. "And thanks for your help with...well, everything, I guess." She glanced down at her bandaged arm appreciatively. "By the way, how long was I out?"

Erik shrugged. "A while."

But it looked like more than a while to Alyssa. Erik's pink cheeks peeled. And dark, sleepless circles lined his eyes.

"After you got hurt, I tore the boat apart, looking for something to give you to help with the pain. I just couldn't–" His voice trailed off. His eyes misted as he looked out to sea.

Alyssa blinked. Couldn't lose me, she thought, finishing for him. Her heart suddenly filled with a flurry of butterflies.

"That's when I found the binoculars and the charts," he added sheepishly. "But I'm glad your fever broke." He swallowed uncomfortably, his voice dropping to a whisper as he muttered, "You were talking a bunch in your sleep."

"I was?" Alyssa's throat suddenly tightened, the warm glow inside her chest instantly fading. She stammered, "Wha — what did I say?"

Erik's lips drew taut as he gave her a noncommittal shrug. But his glance was knowing. Embers of jealousy kindled in his smoky eyes.

Alyssa's face fell. He knew.

Despite her attempts to keep her illicit relationship with Justin a secret until her dying days, she had subconsciously let it slip in her feverish state. And judging by Erik's reaction, she never called for him by name. Not once.

Especially after all he did for her.

Slowly, she reached inside the pocket of her khaki shorts, removing Officer Hidalgo's dolphin pin. The sun glistened off its silvery surface as her thumb rubbed its smooth texture one last time.

She glanced back at Erik, studying her intently. The angry glow in his eyes began to fade as if he imagined the scene she'd encountered in the Command and Control Room aboard the Siren, again reminding him of the loved ones he found lying dead.

Alyssa bit her lip, strengthening her resolve. It's time to move on, she decided, her mind suddenly lucid and determined. Everyone she cared about is gone.

Except for Erik. And if she wanted him to know that for sure, she had to let go of the past.

Willing herself to stand, she clenched the pin inside her fist, cocking her arm back to cast it into the sea, to its final resting place near its deserved owner. Her attempts to honor his death had failed. She would never find his family. His body would never be laid to rest at Arlington National Cemetery. Neither would those of any of the Siren's crew.

Her arm arced through the air, freeing herself from the burden she bore, when Erik caught her wrist mid-swing. The pin fell from her hand, skittering across the open deck.

Alyssa crumbled to her knees, her shoulders heaving with unspoken sorrow.

Silently, Erik picked up the pin and knelt beside her. He placed the silver dolphin fish in the palm of her hand, wrapping her fingers tightly around it. "It's okay to remember," he said softly as he smoothed back her hair.

She squeezed her eyes shut, frustrated by her lack of tears.

Gently, she felt Erik place his lips against each of her closed eyelids, then lace his fingers through her free ones. She looked up at him, studying his expression. His short wave of jealousy had faded, replaced instead with forgiveness and understanding.

"It's okay," he repeated. She saw the pain of loss in his weary gray eyes and the fear he'd harbored wondering if she'd recover. As he wrapped his arms comfortingly around her, the pin dug deep into her palm, reminding her of what she'd left behind. Her head rested against his neck as she closed her eyes sadly...remembering.

After a long moment, Erik whispered, "So what do you think we should do now?"

Alyssa straightened, blinking to clear her thoughts. There would be ample time to remember the dead. But for now, they must tend to their own survival. Several ideas flashed through Alyssa's mind as she surveyed the secluded island:

Their water supply would soon run dangerously low. They should find a fresh water spring to refill their canisters. And set up bowls to collect rainwater.

The end of the hurricane season was still a few weeks away. They should test the cabanas' durability in protecting them from the imminent storms.

After the arduous journey and pirate attack, their boat was in serious need of repair. They should patch the sails and scan the hull for damage and leaks.

Judging by Erik's peeling shoulders and face, they were low on provisions. If the sheds here proved empty, they should set sail again to scour nearby islands for supplies.

Plus, she couldn't remember the last time she'd eaten her fill. They should set up a few fishing lines and search the island for fresh fruits.

Instead, she named the one requirement she knew his body craved most. "You should rest. I'll get started on…something." Though on what exactly, she wasn't sure.

A smile flickered across Erik's lips. "Thanks. I think I'll take you up on that offer." He released her and stretched out across the makeshift bed he'd assembled on the floor of the boat, closing his eyes.

Sitting cross-legged on the bench, Alyssa stared up at the clear sky. A light breeze rustled her disheveled hair. It was hard to believe only a few days had passed since she was trapped inside the Siren, uncertain if she'd ever see the sun again. Harder still to believe what she'd endured since her escape.

She put her hand to the huge lump at the base of her skull, sighing deeply as she gingerly rubbed her head. Her world–the world–would never be the same.

"You doing okay?" Erik looked up, opening one eyelid.

"Yeah…I'm fine. I guess."

Erik grinned knowingly. "Come here," he said, taking her hand to pull her down by him on the floor. He wrapped one arm around her shoulders, keeping her close, then planted a kiss on the top of her matted head.

Everything could wait. They were safe. For now.

Alyssa laid her cheek against his warm, bare chest. And fell instantly asleep.

Debbie Kump

About the Author

    After graduating from Cornell University with degrees in Biology and Education, I taught middle and high school science in Maui, Seattle, and the Twin Cities and worked as a marine naturalist aboard a whale watch and snorkel cruise. I now live in Minnesota with my husband, two sons, and three Siberian huskies. When I'm not writing my next novel, I enjoy coaching my sons' soccer, hockey, lacrosse, and baseball teams and dog sledding my boys to school.

Visit her website:
https://sites.google.com/site/debbiekumpbooks/